Oh What A (Wedding) Night

(Brazen Brides Book 3)

CHERYL BOLEN

Some of the praise for Cheryl Bolen's writing:

"One of the best authors in the Regency romance field today." – *Huntress Reviews*

"Bolen's writing has a certain elegance that lends itself to the era and creates the perfect atmosphere for her enchanting romances." – *RT Book Reviews*

The Counterfeit Countess (Brazen Brides, Book 1)
Daphne du Maurier award finalist for Best Historical Mystery

"This story is full of romance and suspense. . . No one can resist a novel written by Cheryl Bolen. Her writing talents charm all readers. Highly recommended reading! 5 stars!" – *Huntress Reviews*

"Bolen pens a sparkling tale, and readers will adore her feisty heroine, the arrogant, honorable Warwick and a wonderful cast of supporting characters." – *RT Book Reviews*

One Golden Ring (Brazen Brides, Book 2)
"*One Golden Ring*...has got to be the most PERFECT Regency Romance I've read this year." – *Huntress Reviews*

Holt Medallion winner for Best Historical, 2006

Lady By Chance (House of Haverstock, Book 1)
Cheryl Bolen has done it again with another sparkling Regency romance. . .Highly recommended – *Happily Ever After*

The Bride Wore Blue (Brides of Bath, Book 1)
Cheryl Bolen returns to the Regency England she knows so well. . .If you love a steamy Regency with a fast pace, be sure to pick up *The Bride Wore Blue*. – *Happily Ever After*

With His Ring (Brides of Bath, Book 2)
"Cheryl Bolen does it again! There is laughter, and the interaction of the characters pulls you right into the book. I look forward to the next in this series." – *RT Book Reviews*

The Bride's Secret (Brides of Bath, Book 3)
(originally titled *A Fallen Woman)*
"What we all want from a love story...Don't miss it!"
– *In Print*

To Take This Lord (Brides of Bath, Book 4)
(originally titled *An Improper Proposal)*
"Bolen does a wonderful job building simmering sexual tension between her opinionated, outspoken heroine and deliciously tortured, conflicted hero." – *Booklist of the American Library Association*

My Lord Wicked
Winner, International Digital Award for Best Historical Novel of 2011.

With His Lady's Assistance (Regent Mysteries, Book 1)
"A delightful Regency romance with a clever and personable heroine matched with a humble, but intelligent hero. The mystery is nicely done, the romance is enchanting and the secondary characters are enjoyable." – *RT Book Reviews*

Finalist for International Digital Award for Best Historical Novel of 2011.

A Duke Deceived
"*A Duke Deceived* is a gem. If you're a Georgette Heyer fan, if you enjoy the Regency period, if you like a genuinely sensuous love story, pick up this first novel by Cheryl Bolen."
– *Happily Ever After*

Books by Cheryl Bolen

Regency Romance

Brazen Brides Series
   Counterfeit Countess (Book 1)
   One Golden Ring (Book 2)
   Oh What A (Wedding) Night (Book 3)

House of Haverstock Series
   Lady by Chance (Book 1)
   Duchess by Mistake (Book2)
   Countess by Coincidence (Book 3)

The Brides of Bath Series:
   The Bride Wore Blue (Book 1)
   With His Ring (Book 2)
   The Bride's Secret (Book 3)
   To Take This Lord (Book 4)
   Love in the Library (Book 5)
   A Christmas in Bath (Book 6)

The Regent Mysteries Series:
   With His Lady's Assistance (Book 1)
   A Most Discreet Inquiry (Book 2)
   The Theft Before Christmas (Book 3)
   An Egyptian Affair (Book 4)

The Earl's Bargain
My Lord Wicked
His Lordship's Vow
A Duke Deceived

Novellas:
Christmas Brides (3 Regency Novellas)

Inspirational Regency Romance
Marriage of Inconvenience

Romantic Suspense
Texas Heroines in Peril Series:
    Protecting Britannia
    Capitol Offense
    A Cry in the Night
    Murder at Veranda House

Falling for Frederick

American Historical Romance
A Summer to Remember (3 American Historical Romances)

World War II Romance
It Had to be You

Dedication

For AnnMarie Spiby in appreciation of her support of historical romance—and especially for the many things she's done to support my books.

$\mathcal{P}$rologue

At night the invisible line of demarcation between the City of London and its East End became more pronounced as the narrow streets east of Aldgate took on an eerily sinister air. Even the sounds were different here in the East End than those emanating from the solid edifices of The City. Cackles induced by too much gin, incessant crying of unwanted babies, and coarse solicitations from flea-bitten whores were as intrinsic to this neighborhood as its rickety, bulging buildings. Here, human life held no value. Cutthroats would kill a man for two pence.

Which was one reason why William Birmingham never went east of Aldgate at night without a weapon.

On his normal nocturnal forays to the docks where the Birmingham yacht was moored he was accompanied by a virtual army of his family's trusted guards.

Tonight he came alone.

MacIver had requested that he do so. And when thousands of pounds were at stake, William could be commanded, especially since MacIver was one of the few men he trusted.

As William neared the docklands tavern where he would meet MacIver, he patted his coat and was oddly comforted by the steely feel of his pistol. The very threat of danger accelerated the thump of his heartbeat. In a good way. While his brothers made their fortunes taking risks on the stock market or in staid banking circles, William thrived on risking his own life and limb. He courted adventure with the same fervor that guided Nick and Adam to seek ever-higher interest rates. Nothing could induce him to settle down with the family business on Threadneedle Street. Not when he could help the Birmingham coffers in capitals throughout Europe--or in seedy little taverns in London's East End.

The Howling Hound public house—aptly named for its raucous noises—was located a hundred yards from the docks and had long been a favorite haunt of sailors. William circled the tavern's exterior twice, looking for any shadowed figures lurking in doorways. Once he was satisfied he was not walking into a trap, he dismounted to wait outside the tavern for MacIver.

He did not expect danger, but a rich man must be careful in this neighborhood. William had chosen to disguise his wealth by covering his finely tailored clothing with a worn, outmoded greatcoat that did little to protect him from the January chill. He would not, however, concede to riding a nag. Had he need for a fast getaway, he wished to be assured of a fleet-footed beast.

Mellow yellow light from the tavern's window spilled onto the dirt street outside, and the night was filled with the sound of foghorns and cockney voices alternately arguing and laughing lustily. Before two minutes had passed, MacIver came swaggering up to him. Neither man spoke until the gap between them was less than an arm's length.

"'Tis good to see ye've followed me instructions

to a T, Mr. Birmingham," the older man said.

"Only because you've earned my trust."

MacIver's eyes narrowed as he peered into the Howling Hound, then lowered his voice. "Let us move away a wee bit."

The two men strode into the middle of the street. William could barely see his companion's craggy face in the night's misty darkness. "You've got the bullion?"

"Aye, but we've got to be careful. What with the cutthroats and the authorities, a gent can't be too careful."

"Then you won't be able to deliver it to my brother's bank?" William asked.

MacIver shook his head. "Not for this transaction, guv'nah."

William's brows dipped. "Have you not been well paid in the past?"

"Aye, but I'm merely a go-between this time."

This time? William could not believe that MacIver had ever been anything but a go-between, a bridge from the smugglers to the Birminghams, England's wealthiest family. He shrugged. "It's of no importance how we get it to my brother. As you know, my family does not lack for safe conveyances and well-armed guards."

"Aye. That's what will be needed now." MacIver lowered his raspy voice. "This shipment is considerably more valuable than the others."

"How much more valuable?"

"Eighty thousand pounds."

Considerably more valuable, indeed. William tamped down his excitement and spoke casually in his cultured voice. "How do we take possession?"

"Ye must wait until yer contacted."

MacIver's methods had changed. The man had previously been too greedy to trust anyone else. Of course, previous bullion shipments had never exceeded twenty thousand pounds. "And who will be contacting me?" William asked.

"A . . . lady."

"And how will I know this . . . lady?"

"She will be lovely, and her name is Isadore."

$\mathcal{C}$hapter 1

"I'd rather be dead than wed." Lady Sophia glanced down at the solid earth some forty feet below and was sickeningly aware of how close she was to fulfilling her statement. She prayed the ledge upon which she stood would not give way.

"But ye are wed, milady!"

Depend on her pragmatic maid to take things so utterly literally. "Wed, but not bed—and I believe that is a vastly important distinction."

Her maid snorted.

Flattening herself against the wall, Lady Sophia inched toward the corner of the building.

"I'm shaking so hard I fear I'll tumble to me death," Dottie said. "Ye know how fearful I am of heights."

"No one held a pistol to your head and forced you to come out that window with me." Why must she always speak so flippantly in grave situations? Seriously, Sophia wouldn't at all like to see her trusted servant splattered on the gravel simply because she herself had made the dreadful mistake of marrying Lord Finkel that very afternoon.

"I've been with ye since the day ye was born, and I'll not leave ye now. Besides, I didn't want to be around when yer bridegroom discovers ye've fled. The servants say Lord Finkel has a fierce temper."

Finkie? A fierce temper? Sophia could hardly credit it. An affable baboon was closer to the mark. Why, oh why, had she ever consented to wed the bore? Perhaps because he was titled, terribly handsome, paid uncommon homage to her beauty—and had protected her sister's reputation. In what was undoubtedly the most moronic moment of her life she had decided that being Finkie's marchioness was preferable to being a spinster of the advanced age of seven and twenty.

That was before he kissed her. The only physical reaction his most unsatisfactory kiss elicited in her was nausea. Because of the kippers. Lord Finkel's breath smelled—and tasted—distinctly of kippers.

And that bit of knowledge added to the tusk business sent her packing her bags before he had the opportunity to offend any more of her senses.

In all fairness to Lord Finkel, it wasn't his fault about the tusk business. It only happened that once—the day his valet was abed with fever and had been unable to shave the tufts of nasal hair that protruded from each of Finkie's nostrils like a pair of elephant tusks. But still, whenever she thought of Lord Finkel after that she had been unable to dispel the vision of those dark brown tusks jutting from his nose.

All of this made her seem excessively shallow and unduly affected by sensory assaults. Which she really couldn't deny. But there was something else about Finkie that put her off, though she could not express it any more than she understood it. She supposed it all boiled down to the fact that—try as she might—she could not admire the man. He was even more shallow than she!

If she and Dottie could just make it to the corner of the building, they could lower themselves onto the steep roof of the orangery and from there could shimmy down to the shrubs. "Should you like me to hold your hand?" Sophia offered.

Dottie sucked in her breath. "No, please. I beg you, don't touch me!" Her maid's voice quivered with terror.

Curling her toes and gripping the stone wall, Sophia ever so slightly swiveled her head to face Dottie, but the night was so inky black she could not see her. "Then allow me to take your valise— or should I say, Lord Finkel's valise. Then I'll be balanced with a valise in each hand."

"I 'av a better idea."

Her maid's utterance was followed by the distant thump of the valise hitting the ground.

"A very good idea." Lady Sophia let go of her own valise. "Oh, dear," she whispered, "I do hope no one heard the noise."

"If they did look out the window," Dottie said in a low voice, "they'd likely not see anything to rouse suspicion."

Of course. Dottie was always right. (A pity Sophia had not listened to her when she disparaged Lord Finkel.) Anyone who may have heard the noise would be looking for people, which they wouldn't see because these people were still flapping against a wall three floors up.

"You don't suppose his lordship will 'av me arrested for stealing his valise?" Dottie asked.

"I daresay he won't even miss it. Had he need of it, it wouldn't have been just sitting there quite empty in his library. You must own, it looks a bit tawdry for a man of Lord Finkel's extravagant taste."

"Aye, that it does."

Soon Sophia reached the corner of the edifice and negotiated a turn, relieved to see the silvery-looking top of the orangery. She drew a deep breath and lowered herself until she was sitting upon its roof. A moment later, a trembling Dottie joined her. "What now, milady?"

"We're going to scoot to the lowest part, then climb down those yews."

"Ye'll get yer cape filthy -- if ye don't break yer lovely neck."

"Don't be so pessimistic. The hardest part's behind us," Sophia called over her shoulder as she pushed off. Somewhere between the apex of the glass building and the yew trees which skimmed its side, she wondered how long a bridegroom would wait for his bride to prepare for bed. Would Finkie be pounding upon her door yet? Or worse still, would he be using his considerable strength to tear it down? She needed no greater impetus than the vision of her exceedingly strong bridegroom—enraged—to send her sprawling into the yew branches. *Rip.* She winced at the damage to her silk dress but scurried down the tree, grateful her gloves protected her hands.

While Dottie gathered up her courage to follow her mistress, Sophia collected the two valises, but when she returned, Dottie just sat atop the glass building whimpering. "I can't."

Sophia drew an impatient breath. "If I can do it, you can. I assure you, this is a most sturdy tree."

"But it don't have limbs like a proper tree. I fear I'll topple on me head."

"You put your feet first," Sophia said through clenched teeth. "And I beg that you hurry. We really must be away from Upton Manor when Lord Finkel discovers me gone."

The maid eased each dangling leg over the roofline. "I can't."

"Just leap onto the tree and slide down. That tree's not going anywhere. Besides, I'll be right here to catch you if you fall." Sophia came to stand directly beneath her maid.

That seemed to ease Dottie's fears.

A moment later, amid a great deal of whining and gasping, the maid's feet touched solid ground, and the two women began to tread across the frosty grass of Upton Manor.

Sophia sighed, her breath forming a cloud in the frigid air. "A pity I didn't get married in the summer."

"Why do you say that, milady?" Dottie asked, breathlessly.

"Because tonight must be the coldest night of the year."

"Aye, it's blustery, all right, but at least it's not snowing."

"A good thing, too. Our tracks would be devilishly hard to erase in the snow, and I shouldn't like for Lord Finkel to find me and bring me back."

"He's sure to go to the posting inn in Knotworth."

"That is why we shall go to the posting inn *north* of Knotworth. He will, quite naturally, be expecting me to return to London."

"We aren't going to Lunnon?"

"Of course we're going to London."

"Yer too clever for me. Clever ye were, too, to 'av

us dress in black so we'll blend in with the night, but why did you insist on me wearing one of yer lovely gowns?"

"Because Lord Finkel is sure to send servants searching for me, and they will quite naturally be seeking a well-born lady traveling with her maid. I have therefore decided that we will travel as sisters, and I shan't wish for anyone to suspect that I'm anything other than a genteel lady of middle class."

"I won't tell anyone yer a fine lady."

"Of course you won't. You're to be a mute."

"One of them people who can't speak?" There was a smidgeon of outrage in Dottie's voice.

"Precisely."

* * *

He had waited a very long time to make Lady Sophia his own. He could scarcely believe his good fortune. For years every eligible bachelor in the *ton* had begged for her hand in marriage, but it was he who had been so singularly honored. He alone possessed the three things that had endeared himself to the beautiful lady: his title, his good looks, and his ability to protect her sister's good name.

Lady Sophia need never know she had been one of dozens he had duped or betrayed over the years, nor did she need to know his greatest source of income came from his *arrangement* with the publisher Smith. Because of his own exalted position, Lord Finkel possessed all manner of information that wealthy aristocrats would pay handsomely to prevent from being published. The prevention of one particular piece relating to Lady Sophia's younger sister had won him Lady Sophia's profound gratitude.

Now he had what he'd always wanted. His wife was beautiful, came with a large dowry, and in a few minutes he would slake his intense hunger for her between two smooth, ivory thighs.

The very thought aroused him.

But what in the hell was taking her so bloody long to get ready for bed? She had said she would come to his room through the dressing room that linked her chambers to his. During the hour he had waited, he had schooled himself to be patient. He had anticipated this night for years. A few minutes more would not matter.

He strode angrily across the carpet of his bedchamber, yanked the stopper off a decanter of Madeira, poured himself a glass, and drank it in one long swig. This wasn't how he'd planned this night. Knowing his bride was a virgin, he had intended to relax her with a glass of wine as they cozied up on the settee by his fire while he touched her in places that would have her begging to be carried to his bed.

Now the scenario would change.

He was much too hungry for her to waste time on foreplay, and he was so angry that a swift deflowering would give him great pleasure. Cursing under his breath, he began to pace the carpet.

Another half hour passed. Damn, but he could be the gentleman no longer! He rushed to his dressing room and stormed through it, throwing open the door to his wife's bedchamber. His eye went straight to the large tester bed draped in emerald silk. It was empty. His gaze circled the silent room.

Not a soul in sight.

Was the damn wench still in her dressing

room? He stalked to the door and swung it open. The gown she had worn that day puddled on the floor, but neither its owner nor her maid were anywhere in sight.

What the hell? Seized by a blinding fury, he reentered her bedchamber and scanned the sumptuous room. A piece of parchment was propped up on the gilt escritoire. His brows scrunched down, he stalked to the desk and began to read.

Dear Lord Finkel,

I've had a change of heart. I do not wish to be your wife. Please don't try to bring me back. I shall consult with my brother. Perhaps he can propose an agreeable manner in which we can dissolve this marriage. I'm truly sorry.

S.

A scalding, thundering rage bolted through him. He sure as hell *was* going to bring her back! She was his, by God. If he had to rape her, he'd make her his. He returned to his chamber and rang for a servant.

When his puzzled valet appeared, Lord Finkel spit out his orders. "Gather up all the footmen and have them meet me in the library."

He swiftly dressed and went downstairs to the book-lined chamber. As soon as he took a seat behind his desk, he glanced at the floor and realized his valise was not there where he always kept it. His heart pounding, he leaped to his feet and began to search the room. But the bag was gone.

The first servant who entered the room had to bear his wrath. "Who in the hell's taken my gray valise?"

"I couldn't say, my lord."

Lord Finkel pounded his desk. "Throckmorton! Come here at once."

A few seconds later the panting butler entered the library. "My lord?"

"My valise is gone!" Lord Finkel said. "Do you know anything about it?"

"No, my lord."

One of a pair of youthful footmen who came striding into the chamber answered him. "I believe your wife's maid has it, my lord."

"My wife's maid?" Lord Finkel thundered. "Why in the hell didn't you take it from her?"

The footman shrugged. "'Twern't my place. I thought — because it was shabby like — you'd given it to the lady."

He would gladly kill the bitch. And her mistress, too. His mouth set firmly, his voice grim, he appraised the room full of servants. "The woman is a thief. She and . . . Lady Finkel have disappeared with my valise. I want all of them back. Whichever of you finds the . . . *ladies* will be rewarded handsomely."

* * *

Several hours later Sophia and Dottie, so exhausted they could barely set one foot in front of the other, exclaimed at the sight of the welcome lantern glow that illuminated the exterior of the posting inn at the town that must be Shelton. It had been more than two hours since they had seen a single halo of light—not even a carriage lamp, which was really not surprising. Only a lunatic would brave these muddy country roads at night during a wretched rain storm.

More than once during the miserable trek Sophia had asked herself if she would have gone out Lord Finkel's window had she known that she would have to brave so savage a storm. No sooner had they cleared Upton Manor than thunder began to rumble and prodigious amounts of rain started to pound down upon them. Her merino cape was of little protection against the deluge. Indeed, not even the linen shift closest to her body remained dry. Her wet boots rubbed big, raw blisters on her feet. And she had never been so cold in her entire life. Despite all the physical discomforts, though, she thought she would rather be traipsing through a blizzard than be in Lord Finkel's bed — beneath him.

Voices filled the livery stable, and the inn yard was crammed with conveyances. It was just her luck that on the night she fled Finkie's bed the tiny village of Shelton had become a mecca for aborted London-bound travelers. Before she and Dottie even proceeded through the aged timber door of the Prickly Pig, she knew there would not be an available room.

She only hoped they could find a dry spot to wait for the morning post chaise—if the innkeeper did not toss out the pair of bedraggled women. She clutched Dottie's bony forearm. "Remember, you are not to speak." Then she threw open the door.

The blazing fire that warmed the room was a far more welcome sight than the forty or more persons — all men and all gaping at her — who crammed into the small tavern.

She flipped off the hood of her cape and held her head high as she regally strode to an aproned man who looked as if he could be the innkeeper. "My sister and I should like chambers," she said.

Roars of laughter greeted her words. Her first

thought was that everyone knew Dottie was not her sister, but then she realized they could not possibly know such a thing. Therefore, they must be laughing at the improbability of her securing a room on such a night as this.

"I'm sorry, miss. We're full up tonight," the man said in a kindly voice. He no doubt took pity on the deranged woman who stood before him soaked from head to toe.

She sighed. "If you could just secure a dry corner for us to wait until the morning post chaise . . ."

The innkeeper shrugged. "I'm sorry, miss, but this taproom's the only place."

She favored him with a radiant smile. Since she had left the school room (long ago), she had discovered that a smile from Lady Sophia Beresford was as treasured by men as a gift of shiny guineas. As she stood insipidly, her gaze flicked to the jagged tears in her costly cape and to the mud-encrusted boots. She ran a hand through her dark locks. It was rather like petting a wet duck. How perfectly UNappealing she must look! Even if she was flashing her best smile. Heaven help her if he took her for a doxie.

"I'll see if I can find two more chairs," he said, disappearing behind a swinging door.

She drew a sigh of relief that he'd not thought her a loose woman.

A moment later he returned with a spindleless chair in each hand. "I'll sit you ladies in the corner and bring you some 'ot tea."

"We would be exceedingly grateful," Sophia said.

During the next hour as she sat there unable to talk to Dottie because of Dottie's orders not to reply, Lady Sophia took the opportunity to observe the drunken men who surrounded them. They must be servants of the persons of quality who no doubt were fast asleep in comfortable beds upstairs. Though she was seven and twenty years of age and considered herself a woman of the world, Sophia had never before been in a room full of low-born men.

At the very instant she came to that realization, an exceedingly well-dressed man came striding into the taproom, with an older, less elegantly dressed man tagging behind him. No doubt, his valet. The younger man tossed off his dripping great coat, handed it to his servant, and scanned the room, his gaze flitting past Sophia before he made eye contact with the innkeeper and began to address him.

The room was so noisy Sophia could not hear what the man said, but she could not seem to remove her gaze from him. Without the enormous coat, he was uncommonly handsome. Though he was a gentleman from his starchy cravat to the tips of his shiny Hessians (which, unlike Sophia's boots, were *not* muddy), there was a ruggedness about him. She could see him striding the bow of a pirate ship with broadsword in hand, his golden hair waving in the breeze, his exceedingly wide shoulders straining against a creamy linen shirt. His skin glowed with a healthy summer-like tan despite that it was the dead of winter.

She watched as the innkeeper solemnly shook his head, and the handsome newcomer nodded. A moment later, still standing at the bar, he tossed down a bumper of ale.

To keep from staring at the handsome man, she lifted the curtain to peer out the window. Her heart nearly exploded at what she saw. Two men whose Finkel livery showed beneath their gaping coats were handing their horses to an ostler. "Come, Dottie, quickly," she commanded as she whipped out of her chair and strode to the bar to stand beside the Adonis. "Well met, sir. I've been searching for you," she said boldly to the well dressed man.

He set down his drink and turned to regard her. She was careful to keep her back to the door while yanking Dottie's arm so that she would do the same. Remembering her torn clothing, she prayed he would not mistake her for a trollop.

His very green eyes raked over her, and it was a moment before he replied. "Then you must be Isadore."

It was several seconds before she found her voice. "Indeed I am, and this is my elder sister, Dorothea, who is a mute."

She prayed Isadore was *not* a trollop.

$\mathcal{C}$hapter 2

Though the two ladies did not resemble each other at all, William could more easily have believed the mute to be mother rather than sister to Isadore, whom he judged to be five and twenty years of age. At first he had not noticed the younger woman's beauty behind the mud, ragged clothing, and disheveled hair. It wasn't until she stood before him, speaking in her cultured voice, that he really looked at her and discovered the lovely face peeking out from the soggy mass of dark hair. His penetrating gaze took in her creamy skin, teeth that were as even and white as a blanket of snow, and huge chocolate eyes that were fringed with long, dark lashes. The woman was remarkably pretty.

For two weeks now he had been expecting to cross paths with the lovely Isadore but never imagined they would meet on a frigid night in a village far removed from London, a village whose name he could not even recall. Yet the moment he realized how beautiful this woman was, he was certain he had finally met Isadore.

Then he doubted himself. How could she possibly have known he'd be forced to stop in this wretched village because of a tumultuous rain storm? Of course, were it not raining, he would likely have needed to change horses here. She must have known this. She might even have been following him.

He was in a quandary as to what to expect now. Surely she did not have the bullion with her. And surely her frail looking sister was unaware of Isadore's dealings with smugglers. It was imperative that they find a place to talk in private. "Would that I could offer you ladies a private parlor, but we are told that is impossible tonight."

"As we have already discovered, sir," Isadore answered.

"There just might be a way . . ." he began. "If you ladies will pardon me. . ." He bent to whisper in his valet's ear, and the man departed.

A few moments later, a smiling Thompson returned and bent to whisper in his master's ear.

"If you ladies would be so kind as to come with us," William said, striding toward his servant. "I believe my man has been able to *persuade* the inn's proprietor to part with his private chambers for a few hours."

"We'll need to fetch our valises," Isadore said, giving him a pleading look with those large, sultry eyes of hers.

William nodded at Thompson.

"Allow me to retrieve them, ladies," the valet said.

Turning her face only slightly, Isadore directed him to the corner where two valises reposed in a wet puddle. "Thank you," she told Thompson.

William could not tear his gaze from the lovely lady, especially since she had turned her head so stiffly. Was there something wrong with her? At least there was nothing wrong with her mind. This woman certainly had learned how and when to use her not-insignificant beauty to get exactly what she wanted from men. Is that how she had acquired the bullion?

As they strolled into the rooms located behind the kitchen, the innkeeper apologized profusely for the untidiness of his private chambers which consisted of a small, fire-lit parlor and an adjoining bedchamber.

"It is of no significance," William said, eying the cluttered table tops and the rumpled bed in the next room. "I merely wished to provide a private, dry place for my . . . sisters, to change into dry attire, and perhaps get a bit of sleep. Clean linens are all that are required."

While a plump woman made the bed, he directed his attention to Isadore. "Do you have everything you will need?"

Her gaze flicked to the saturated valises. "I fear all our clothing is damp, but I shall be very glad to be out of these clothes and am most grateful to you."

"Then I will leave you ladies now," he said, "but I'll return in half an hour to see if I can be of any further service." *And try to find out about the bullion.*

Those long lashes of hers dipped seductively. "You've been enormously helpful."

When he and Thompson returned thirty minutes later, he momentarily thought he'd come to the wrong room. Not only had it been miraculously tidied, but all the furnishings had been rearranged. Seating surfaces that had once faced the fireplace were now turned away from it, presumably to shield their occupants' vision away from the assortment of feminine garments that hung on racks strewn before the fire.

Isadore herself looked vastly different. Her mahogany coloured hair—now dry—was arranged in a stylish Grecian sweep, and she had donned a sapphire gown that, while wrinkled and damp, was of very fine quality. And she freely moved her person and her head, dispelling his earlier suspicion that something was wrong with her neck.

MacIver's description did not do the woman justice. She was stunning.

In half an hour she had transformed from a shadowy figure of dubious repute into something of a well-born lady. Not, of course, that Isadore could precisely be a lady. Ladies did not secure gold bullion from smugglers.

She was more of an enigma than ever. Her gown and hairstyle indicated that she moved in fashionable circles, yet she had obviously taken charge of housekeeping and hair-arranging chores that were normally executed by a maid. Beauty notwithstanding, Isadore was resourceful, tidy, not without modesty, and was somewhat well bred. So why in the devil was she brokering gold bullion?

Even if she had mastered the use of sultry glances and purring voice to get what she wanted from men, William could not dislike her. "Should you ladies care for something to eat? Or drink?" he asked.

"We're fine," Isadore said, "except for being exhausted."

William placed his boot inside the door. He and Thompson crossed the wooden floor and dropped onto sofa cushions flattened by many years of use. "You might be fine now, but I would wager this has been a difficult night for you. Have you ladies been in Shelton long?" He had finally learned the name of this village whose only reason for existence had to be to provide food, drink, and fresh horses for northern-bound travelers.

"We arrived just before you," Isadore said with a shrug. "We met with a bit of misfortune."

Good lord! Had highwaymen stolen the bullion? His brows lowered. "What kind of misfortune? You didn't lose the . . . *commodity* that I seek?"

Her lashes whisked against her cheeks. "No, but we were forced to walk here after . . ."

Dear god, highwaymen *had* taken the bullion!

". . . after the gentleman we were riding with tried to take certain liberties."

Dorothea's eyes rounded, and she nodded in confirmation.

A lovely woman like Isadore had likely spent many a year fighting off men's advances. He pitied the sister whose misfortunes were even more cruel when contrasted with her fortunate sibling. "Then you must allow me to escort you ladies to your destination," he said.

Isadore bestowed a lovely smile upon him. "That would be exceedingly kind of you."

"Your destination is?" he asked.

"The same place as yours, I believe."

"London?"

She nodded.

William's gaze circled the gathering. "I should like to present my valet to you ladies. Thompson is a devilishly handy man to have about."

Thompson did not meet the ladies' gazes when he answered. "You mustn't believe everything Mr. Birmingham says."

"You're much too modest," Isadore told the valet. "You were most resourceful in procuring our rooms." Then she gave William a knowing smile.

He wished like the devil she wouldn't smile like

that at him. Made it difficult to remember what he was going to say. And there were several matters he had wished to bring up. He cleared his throat. "I feel deuced awkward calling you ladies by your Christian names."

Isadore gave him a blank stare.

"You are possessed of a surname?" he asked.

She favored him with a fetching smile. "Of course."

Well? It was too much to hope that her intelligence matched her considerable beauty. "Your surname is?"

"It's a frightfully silly name, if you must know," she finally said, flicking her gaze to her mute sister, who nodded.

He eyed them with skepticism. "I cannot believe anything about you ladies could be silly."

"We're Doors."

His brows lowered over suddenly narrowed eyes. *Imbeciles more likely.*

"Dorothea Door and Isadore Door. You see, I told you our names are silly."

Their parents were either mentally deficient or possessed of a wicked sense of humor, but a gentleman could hardly give voice to such suspicions. He racked his brain for something complimentary to say. "There's a certain . . . alliteration about the names."

"Indeed there is. Our brother is Dorian."

Dorian Door? Poor fellow. Exceedingly wicked of the parents. Will stood. "We will leave you ladies. Hopefully, you can get a few hours of rest before we push off in the morning."

Isadore rose. "It's beastly unfair that we shall lie upon a cozy bed while you gentleman are forced to remain in the taproom."

"Don't spare another thought on us. I slept an inordinate amount at my sister's in the north," William said, "and am happy to engage in some camaraderie with other men."

* * *

As exhausted as she had been the previous night/morning, Sophia awakened as the first light of dawn streamed through the window. How odd it seemed to be lying next to her maid. Though she had seen Dottie nearly every day of her life, treating her as an equal was a novel experience. Sophia shifted her weight to the elbow closest to Dottie, looked down at the still-sleeping woman, and nudged her.

Dottie bolted up. "Dear me! 'Tis daylight. We must be getting dressed for the day." Not accustomed to lying about in the mornings, the maid tossed off the covers, strode straight to the chimney, and began to stoke the fire. After it was going she carefully dislodged their clothing from the drying racks. "A pity ye can't wear this black silk no more. 'Twas that wretched yew tree that ruined yer gown." She gathered up Sophia's shift, stays, and stockings and brought them to her mistress.

"Don't fuss over me," Sophia said. "You need to get yourself dressed. I'm perfectly capable of dressing myself."

Dottie snorted. "I hope the 'andsome man don't think I'm too high in the instep."

"I doubt Mr. Birmingham has given you a thought," Sophia said, instantly ashamed of herself for her wicked snobbishness.

"Not that one! Mr. Thompson."

Mr. Thompson? Oh, yes, Sophia realized. The valet. This unplanned journey of hers was giving a fresh skew to her lifetime of disinterest in servants. She not only treated her maid like a family member, but she had also shared a room with a gentleman's valet. Were she pressed to do so, though, Sophia did not believe she could actually recognize Thompson were she to see him on a street.

How could anyone notice the elder man when his master was so exceedingly handsome?

She wiggled from beneath the covers, dangled her feet over the side of the bed, and began to don her woolen stockings. Visions of Mr. Birmingham clouded her thinking. Thank goodness she had finally learned his name. She had begun to despair that his valet would never address his master by his given name. If she--or that blasted Isadore--had some connection to the man, she really ought to know his name.

It would be even more helpful to know the man's connection to Isadore.

Who in the devil was Isadore? Were she a doxy, he would have shared the bedchamber. The very thought of lying naked beside Mr. Birmingham's ruggedly muscled body made her throb in places that were prudently ignored during waking hours.

Finkie had certainly never been able to tap into them.

Why was it she had never met Mr. Birmingham before? He was a gentleman, and judging from the obviously hefty bribe he'd offered the innkeeper, Mr. Birmingham not only was possessed of very deep pockets, but was also used to getting whatever he wanted.

She tried to remember if she had ever known of an exceedingly wealthy Mr. Birmingham and suddenly realized she *had*. Nicholas Birmingham, who had won Lady Fiona Hollingsworth's hand in marriage. It was said the Birmingham Cits were the wealthiest family in England. But this man could not belong to that family. Nicholas Birmingham, who was sinfully handsome himself, looked nothing like this Mr. Birmingham. Nicholas was quite tall, quite lean, and quite dark. This Mr. Birmingham's height was only average. He was *not* lean. And he was not dark. Except for the tan.

A deep melancholy settled over Sophia. Why did she feel like this when she was exceedingly happy to have escaped from Lord Finkel's marital bed? Then it hit her—the reason for her moroseness. That the Finkel servants had come to Shelton in search of her indicated that Finkie wanted her back. He had ignored her plea.

He wanted her for his wife even if she didn't want him. She settled back and pondered that for a moment. It was a perfectly wicked manner for a gentleman to behave. In fact, no true gentleman would ever behave in such a manner, which meant . . . Finkie was wicked.

Only a wicked man would try to force a woman to his bed.

She cringed at the thought of lying with him.

Were his servants promised hefty bribes to bring her back to him? The very notion was like acid boiling into her membranes.

She could never go back to him.

Now she realized how thoroughly she had misjudged him. She had plighted her life to his in gratitude for his protection of Maryann's reputation. But now that she knew how evil he was, she also wondered if he had been more the one who uncovered the unsavory bits than the suppressor of the unsavory bits of her sister's actions.

Now she knew she could not stand up to Finkie alone.

Now, she must disclose all to her brother, who had recently become head of their household.

"Ye can't believe how 'ard it is not to be able to talk," Dottie said. She had retired to a corner of the room to change into one of Sophia's old dresses. It was really rather fortuitous that they were the same size, given the fact they shared no other resemblance besides their height, which was perfectly average. Where Sophia was generously curved, Dottie was as straight as a poker.

Sophia tossed a glance her way. "I'm very proud of you. I know it cannot be easy."

"Can mute people laugh?"

"I don't believe so. Why?"

"I almost burst out laughing when ye said we was the Doors."

Sophia shook her head remorsefully. "It was the best I could come up with. I'm not especially good at thinking on my feet, so to speak."

"Dorothea Door, indeed! The gent's apt to think yer parents are dicked in the nobs."

"I'm afraid I've gotten us into a pickle—or several pickles, actually," Sophia said with a sigh, leaving the bed and coming to stand before the fire as she dressed.

"Better pickled than shackled to Finkel. Never did like the fellow."

"A pity I didn't listen to you."

"Now that Mr. Birmingham . . . I could see ye shackled to someone like him."

Sophia gave a nervous little laugh. "Mr. Birmingham could be a highwayman for all we know."

Dottie shook her head emphatically. "He's a fine gentleman—and wealthy, too. Mark me words." She settled a green shawl over her shoulders and eyed Sophia. "I thought when ye first approached 'im last night that ye knew 'im. Ye spoke as if ye did."

"I was desperate, and he was the only well-bred man in the vicinity. It was imperative that you and I looked as if we were with him. After I saw Finkie's servants out the window, I'd have said or done anything to endear myself to the gentleman."

Dottie snorted. "Ye'd go from the fryin' pan into the fire." She contemplated Sophia from beneath lowered brows. "Who do ye suppose Isadore is?"

"Would that I knew. The only thing I know about her is that Mr. Birmingham has never met her before."

"One thing's for sure," Dottie said as she began to gather up their clothes, neatly fold them, and pack them into their valises. "Ye must look like her."

A knock sounded at the door. Her eyes wide, Sophia placed her index finger to her mouth. "It must be Mr. Birmingham."

She crossed the room and opened the door.

He looked devastatingly handsome—smiling, freshly shaven with a starchy white cravat knotted beneath his tanned face, and he held a tray with a steaming teapot and a rack of toast. "I've brought you ladies something to break the fast."

She widened the door opening. "You, Mr. Birmingham, are a most welcome sight. Do come in."

He set the tray on a table near the window and went to stand in front of the fire. "You, Miss Door, are an even more agreeable sight this morning."

She only then glanced out the window and realized the rain had finally swept by, leaving a lingering mist and roads that looked like swamps. "You are much too kind, sir."

"Will you ladies be ready to leave once you've eaten?"

She spun around to face him. "But the roads . . ."

"I'll own, the going will be slow, but I have great confidence in my coachman. Besides, I'm anxious to be back in London."

How fortunate that London was his destination. "Not nearly as anxious as I, Mr. Birmingham." Leaving the sanctuary of the inn would be one of the most difficult things she'd ever done, for she felt in her bones that Finkie's servants would be watching for her.

Moments later Thompson came and fetched the ladies' bags, and a moment after that, skirts gathered in her hands, she was teetering along a dry plank to Mr. Birmingham's expensive carriage.

Terrified that Finkie's servants would be watching, she pulled down the cape's hood so that it would obstruct her face and hair. As he assisted her into the coach, she caught a glimpse of a man in Finkel livery standing beside the mews, eying them. Her stomach dropped as she climbed into the coach.

Dare she hope she was not recognized? Would not her party look like two pairs of married couples? She sighed. *Dear God, I hope so.*

She and Dottie sat on the front-facing seat, Mr. Birmingham and his servant opposite them. As the carriage slugged through the muddy inn yard, she lifted the maroon velvet curtain and watched in sickening dread as the Finkel servant mounted his horse and began to follow them.

He and three others.

A heavy moroseness settled over her as they reached the road and began to head south. Despite her plea, Lord Finkel meant to get her back. The disgusting thing was, in the eyes of the law, she belonged to him. Like chattel. Or cattle. Or an old rug one meant to tread upon.

Even though it had been some years ago, she still recalled the chilling accounts of Lord Wapping's cruelty to his unfortunate wife. Not even the lady's father had been able to help her.

Like her, Sophia realized with a sickening chill, Lady Wapping had brought a large dowry to her marriage.

Once they cleared the village and were on open, lonely roads she found herself lifting away the velvet curtain, searching for Finkie's servants. She was beginning to believe she had eluded them.

Then, twenty minutes after they left Shelton, she heard an explosion followed immediately by a vile string of curses from Mr. Birmingham's coachman as he drove faster, and the pounding of other horse hooves drew alongside them. "Highwaymen!" the coachman yelled.

Not highwaymen, she thought. Lord Finkel's men, who no doubt had been promised lucrative rewards for restoring Lady Finkel to her bridegroom.

$\mathcal{C}$hapter 3

At the sound of a heavy thump upon the coachman's box, Sophia—and Dottie—screamed at once. One of Finkie's men had leaped upon the coach to do battle with Mr. Birmingham's driver!

The vehicle lurched to a stop.

In a swift and fluid move, both Mr. Birmingham and his valet lunged toward the ladies, then quickly twisted back around to throw up the seat cushions and the hinged seat top. Sophia's thundering heart lifted when she saw the arsenal of weapons stashed beneath the men's seat.

Before her companions could put their hands on the pistols or sabers, the coach door flew open. Then the other door. On either side, menacing-looking men in Finkel livery faced them, their muskets aimed at the passengers.

A sturdily built blond directed his attention at Mr. Birmingham. "We won't 'arm you. All we want is the women."

To Sophia's complete astonishment, Mr. Birmingham leaped onto the armed man, kneeing him in the groin. As all eyes turned on them, Thompson dove into the box for a sword.

Her heart hammering profusely, Sophia watched in horror as Mr. Birmingham and the blond, whose weapon had dropped to the muddy ground, began to pummel each other viciously.

Then her gaze pivoted to the opposite side of

the carriage as Thompson brought up a sword and plunged it into the intruder's side. Her horrified gaze swept to the injured man, who groaned and cursed as crimson began to stain his coat. As he fell backward, his musket exploded, ripping into the top of the coach and sending great clouds of hot powder into the air.

All the while another commotion was taking place outside the carriage as the coachman fought off another man.

She was too terrified to move, too terrified to even scream. Her head bobbed from one side to the other as she watched her courageous companions try to wear down their enemies. As soon as Thompson's profusely bleeding opponent collapsed, another man leaped toward the valet, a dagger in his hand.

Sophia could not watch. She turned away and saw that her gallant Mr. Birmingham was rolling in the mud with the blond, grunting and hissing, and causing her heart to pound prodigiously. She would feel ever so wretched if he sustained serious injury. Because she had foolishly married the wrong man.

Then she got an idea. Her brother had taught her to use a musket! She lunged forward and found a musket which she quickly began to load. But which man would she save? Mr. Birmingham or his valet?

Since Mr. Birmingham's opponent was no longer armed, she decided to aid the brave valet. Aiming her weapon at the man with the dagger, she shouted, "Put down your knife, or I'll fire!"

He turned black eyes on her, lowered his shocked gaze to the musket, then dropped his dagger.

Thompson swiftly picked it up and thanked her.

"Quick, Dottie!" she said. "Your sash! We must tie up this man."

A trembling Dottie obliged by removing her sash and lowering herself from the carriage to aid the valet.

Then Sophia trained her musket on the blond who was doing his best to harm the noble Mr. Birmingham, but the latter had the audacity to look up at her and laugh! "I'll need no rescuing from a woman."

With that comment, Mr. Birmingham shoved his opponent's face into the mud, came to his feet, and planted a muddy boot on the blond's back. Though the blond man was huge, he brought to mind an infant as he lay there kicking and screaming while his limbs flailed about in the mud.

Indeed, she had no cause to come to Mr. Birmingham's assistance. Her mouth gaping open, she eyed the man to whom she owed so much. His sturdy hand wiped over his face to reveal two emerald eyes flashing in cakes of mud. His disheveled golden hair was streaked with mud, and she would vow that the impeccably clothed man had never been more filthy in his privileged life.

And in her very privileged life, she had never seen a more magnificent creature!

Removing her own sash, she came to him and held it out. "Should you like to tie up the man?"

"A very good idea." He took the blue satin. "You stand on his back while I do the honors."

Without a care to the mud that ringed the hem of her dress, she complied. As she watched Mr.

Birmingham outmaneuver the squirming man, her admiration for him grew.

When he finished, he hurried to assist the coachman and quickly knocked that assailant to the ground.

A few minutes later, she surveyed the damage. Three men in Finkel livery were tied with women's sashes, and a fourth lay in the mud clutching his bleeding side while speaking in a most incoherent (though vile) manner. The top of Mr. Birmingham's costly carriage had been all but blown off, and his wonderfully brave servants were hobbling about in a wretched mire of silt.

She felt dreadfully guilty. She was the cause of all this. Innocent people had been put in jeopardy because she had made a horrible mistake. Had her valiant Mr. Birmingham been wounded or—heaven help her—killed, she would have perished on the spot. Or entered a convent to spend the rest of her life trying to atone for her wickedness.

Thank goodness she would be spared that.

His eyes sparkling with mischief, Mr. Birmingham met her gaze. "A bit of mud won't hurt my carriage." He assisted her in one door while Thompson gave his hand to Dottie, who climbed in the other side.

After the coach started moving, Mr. Birmingham lowered his brows and spoke. "Did I or did I not hear Miss Dorothea Door scream? Earlier?"

Sophia and Dottie exchanged worried glances. "I can explain," Sophia said, her heart racing as she tried to come up with a plausible explanation. But just as it had done the night before when he inquired about their surname, her mind was not cooperating.

"And?" he asked.

She heaved a big sigh. Then she thought of something. "My dear sister could once speak, you see. Before the terrible accident that happened before I was born. Ever since poor Dorothea has been mute. She does possess the ability to cry and to scream, but she positively cannot seem to make herself say words." Sophia slid back against the velvet squabs and prayed he would pry no more.

Her prayers went unheeded. "What," he asked, "was the nature of the unfortunate accident?"

She shook her head, biding for time. "It was perfectly dreadful." *But how, you idiot?* she asked herself. Then a most agreeable explanation came to mind. "You see, Dorothea was once a twin. She and her twin sister spoke to each other with ease in a language that was peculiar unto them. Then one day, the sister was struck by lightning. She died on the spot." Sophia turned to Dottie and took her hand. "Poor Dottie was right there. And since that day has been unable to utter another word."

"How dreadful," Thompson said, shooting a most sympathetic look at the poor mute. Or the woman he thought was a mute.

Mr. Birmingham looked exceedingly contrite. "Forgive me for bringing up such a sad recollection," he said.

They rode on in silence for a considerable length of time when he asked, "What was the twin's name?"

What a peculiar request! Then Sophia remembered her parents' alleged propensity for alliteration. "Dorcas."

A smile curved his lip.

Once her nerves had settled, she turned her

thoughts to the supremely handsome man who sat across from her. He definitely was *not* what he seemed. A fine gentleman did not travel about with an arsenal beneath his carriage seat or with a valet who was as adept with a saber as he was with a hot iron. Just who was this Mr. Birmingham and what was the source of his wealth? Not many men would display such a lack of concern when an expensive carriage had to be replaced.

Whatever he did, she was sure it was something unlawful.

Isadore would know. Her insides lurched.

Isadore was up to no good.

* * *

Given that he often traveled with large amounts of money, William's unwritten credo was to always be prepared to thwart attacks, even on a harmless trip to Yorkshire supposedly to visit his sister, Lady Agar. But this latest attack was altogether different. He was not transporting money or gold. He was not protected by loyal Birmingham guards. And he was not the target.

The single-minded abductors were willing to dismiss one of the wealthiest men in England in order to get their hands on Miss Isadore Door and her eighty thousand pounds worth of bullion.

Though he and Thompson had faced down far more ferocious assaults than today's, William had never before fought with such intensity. He had never before wished to protect anything as fiercely as he wished to protect Miss Door.

If that was her name. He was almost certain it could not be.

Even though she had brought such peril upon herself, he was seized with a need to protect her.

He would never forget the terror that spiked through him when the men said they wanted only the women. It would have been easier to hand over a hundred thousand pounds worth of bullion than to allow those men to accost the lovely Isadore.

His gaze whisked over her as she sat across from him, staring intently out the carriage window. How could such an elegant creature be involved with gold smugglers?

The woman was hiding something from him. Was she also shielding her sister from knowledge of her dangerous connections?

Though last night he had determined not to bring up the bullion until he was alone with Isadore, he wavered now. Could he not discuss it in general terms that her mute sister might not understand? In case the sister was not involved in the shady activity.

He cleared his throat.

Isadore turned those large, near black, eyes on him.

"I don't like that a lady is taking such grave risks with her safety," he said.

Their gazes locked, and she did not answer for a moment. "Perhaps the lady has a propensity to act impetuously."

His eyes narrowed. "And regret her impetuous actions afterward?"

She nodded, and he noticed the auburn glints that highlighted her dark hair in daylight.

In that instant his conviction that she was well born was confirmed. For reasons unknown to him, she had decided to embroil herself in this unsavory business in order to lay her hands on a great deal of money.

"I would like to think that once this transaction is closed," he said, "the lady will take her 'rewards' and retire from risky propositions." Then it occurred to him that he did not wish for her to close this transaction. He did not like to think of her doing anything further that might jeopardize that lovely neck of hers.

"Then you and I are in perfect agreement, Mr. Birmingham."

"If it's the money, I'm a very wealthy man . . ."

She stiffened. "I won't accept your money."

She was entirely too proud. Rather than accept a gift from him, she would risk her life. His hands fisted. "Then I'm not letting you out of my sight until the 'transaction' is completed. You're in grave danger."

"Just what are you suggesting, sir?"

"You—and your sister—will stay at my home until I'm assured that you're out of danger."

She shook her head. "I'm . . . an unmarried woman."

The very suggestion of impropriety stirred his lust for her. She was an unmarried woman, a very beautiful unmarried woman, and he was an unmarried man. He had never been more aware of a woman. A sizzling heat flared between them as he drank in her sensuous loveliness, as his heated gaze poured over her exquisite face, down the creamy flesh of her neck and the tops of her breasts swelling against the blue gown.

Bringing a well born lady to his house was not a good idea. How would he be able to stay away from her bed?

He drew a deep breath. "I give you my word to behave as a gentleman. And my servants are very discreet. Your reputation will not suffer."

Her eyes sparkled with mirth. "How can I know you're a gentleman? I know of no gentlemen whose valets are skilled swordsmen." Her gaze darted to Thompson, whose face was inscrutable.

William shrugged. "The manner in which I conduct my business and the manner in which I live in polite society are two completely different things."

"I may regret it, Mr. Birmingham," she said, "but I'm willing to put myself in your hands. Until this business is completed."

* * *

"Four of you couldn't overtake two men?" Lord Finkel thundered.

"Three, counting the coachman," the blond footman said.

"'Twern't just any two men, either," his companion said. "These men was exceedingly well armed."

"And skilled pugilists," a third servant added.

"And mighty handy with a sword, too," a fourth servant said.

Lord Finkel's glare scorched. His bloody wife had gone traipsing off with another man. On his wedding night! How could that be? He had learned that she had met the wealthy bloke at the posting inn at Shelton. Were she running off with another man, would he not have picked her up outside the gates of Upton Manor? "What was the man's name?"

The three men shrugged. "We don't know, my lord," the blond said.

"But he was very rich," the other said.

"His carriage was even finer than yer lordship's."

Lord Finkel's bushy brows lowered. "There was

a crest?"

His servants shook their heads.

"What did the man look like?" Lord Finkel asked.

"He was a very large man," the blond said. "I fought 'im with all me strength, but I was no match for 'im. A giant he was."

The smaller servant nodded. "And his clothes were of very fine quality. Every bit as expensive as yer lordship's."

Lord Finkel pounded upon his desk. "You're to return to Shelton and make inquiries. I need the man's name. Don't come back without it."

"Yes, yer lordship."

* * *

Sophia had thought physical discomfort could get no worse than it had been the night before when she and Dottie had stumbled through a violent rainstorm for six long miles.

She had been wrong.

The five-hour journey to London in Mr. Birmingham's now-topless coach was worse — chiefly because the skies had once again erupted, rendering the interior of his carriage as wet as a pond, a freezing pond that no amount of togetherness made tolerable. She longed to wash the mud from her body. She longed for dry clothing and the warmth of a fire. But most of all, she longed to be on solid ground and rid of the horrid motion sickness that threatened with every turn of the wheels to dislodge the churning contents of her stomach.

When she began to recognize familiar streets in London's West End, an odd sense of comfort stole over her. Comfort mingled with fear. Mr. Birmingham would do his best to disengage her from Dottie in order to demand information that only the mysterious Isadore possessed.

She must not allow herself to be alone with him.

As the carriage turned onto Grosvenor Square, Mr. Birmingham announced that they had arrived at his home. An impressive address. Her great aunt, Lady Gresham, lived there at Number 12.

"Perhaps, sir," Sophia said, "you might wish to enter through the back."

A devilish smile broke over his face. "A very good suggestion, Miss Door," he said. "Were my neighbors to see so bedraggled a man from so bedraggled carriage enter my house, they would be certain to send for the Watch. And we couldn't have that, could we, Miss Door?"

He instructed the coachman to drive to the rear entrance.

What an enigma this man was! His home was among the finest in London, yet she'd never heard of him. She was almost certain the source of his wealth must be illegal. Why else the arsenal in his coach? Why would he be desirous of meeting a strange woman named Isadore for the purpose of exchanging a "commodity"?

A moment later they were disembarking from the carriage, Mr. Birmingham offering Sophia a wet hand. As soon as they stepped into the gracious house, he began to bark orders to his servants to put the sisters into the Blue Room and Yellow Room respectively and to hasten with baths for the ladies.

"What about yourself, Mister Birmingham?" the housekeeper asked, her shocked gaze lingering on her employer's torn, muddy clothes.

"I shall avail myself of one once the ladies are

finished."

As London houses went, especially those on Grosvenor Square, Mr. Birmingham's was small. As befitted a bachelor. Sophia's chest tightened. He was a bachelor, was he not? A lump the size of a walnut lodged in her throat as she climbed the stairs behind him. "Is there. . . a Mrs. Birmingham?" she asked. *Please say no.*

"You will be staying in her room."

The queasiness returned to Sophia's stomach.

"My mother visits once or twice a year. My sister used to occasionally stay in the Yellow Room, but she is married now and has her own house in town."

"Is that the sister you were just visiting in the north?" Sophia asked, her step lightening.

"Yes." He opened the door to the blue chamber, a high-ceilinged room carpeted in pale blue, its walls covered in silk of the same shade. The room bespoke impeccable taste from its high, velvet-draped tester bed to its marble chimney piece centered with a gold clock and flanked by turquoise Sevres vases. Whatever illegal activities Mr. Birmingham engaged in certainly paid handsomely.

"Your sister will have the next room," he said, still standing in the doorway as a pair of footmen carried the slipper tub into the room and placed it in front of the chimney, where a maid was kneeling down to start the fire. "I beg that you ladies join me in the dining room at six," he added.

That would give them three hours to clean, rest, then dress for dinner. "It will be our pleasure," Sophia said.

* * *

Before Sophia and Dottie made their way to the dining room, Sophia demanded two things of her maid. "First," she said to Dottie, who had sneaked to her room to help her dress, "you are *not* to wait upon me."

"Not even to help with yer 'air?"

"Not even to help with my hair. You're to pretend to be a gentlewoman yourself."

Dottie nodded. "A deaf gentlewoman."

"Not deaf. Mute."

"I always get them two mixed up."

All the more reason for Sophia to congratulate herself for demanding that Dottie play the mute. "There is another thing I must ask of you."

Dottie arched her brows.

"You're not to allow me to be alone with Mr. Birmingham."

"You're that attracted to him, eh? If ye ask me, it would be a very good plan if ye let 'im ruin ye so ye wouldn't have to go back to that odious Lord Finkel."

There was merit in what her maid said. If Sophia had a mind to ruin herself with a man she could not think of a more worthy candidate than the sublime Mr. Birmingham. A pity he was a criminal. "That's not what I mean! I cannot be alone with Mr. Birmingham because then he will expect me to be Isadore."

"But he already thinks ye are Isadore!"

"What I mean is that he will endeavor to extract information from me that I cannot possibly produce."

Dottie rubbed her pointy chin. "I can see where that might pose a problem, but what do you care what Mr. Birmingham thinks? Now that he's brought us to Lunnon, why don't ye just return to

Lord Devere's house?"

Sophia had to admit that Dottie was possessed of a great deal of common sense. "I had originally planned to return to my brother's, but now that I know Finkie will do the most vile things in order to keep me shackled to him, I cannot go back to Devere's. Lord Finkel will expect me to go there, and I'm almost certain he will demand that I return to Upton Manor with him." Her shoulders sagged. "And the pity of it is that the law is on his side. You remember the case of Lady Wapping?"

Dottie nodded sadly. "I fear yer right, milady."

"Another very good reason for you to be mute. You'd be certain to slip and call me *my lady*."

"What if that 'andsome Mr. Birmingham comes to yer chamber when yer sleeping?"

The idea of any of her seven and forty previous suitors coming to her bedchamber would have been repugnant, but strangely, the idea of His Sublimeness coming to her bedchamber sent searing quivers over her body. It was difficult for her to even remember the topic Dottie had initiated when thoughts of Mr. Birmingham awakening her with sultry kisses competed. She had to catch her breath before she could answer. "I shall be sick. I will take to my bed with a feigned fever immediately after dinner, and you must pretend to nurse me through the night." Once more Sophia would experience the oddity of sleeping with her servant.

"How I wish I could be taking dinner with the upper servants," Dottie lamented as they moved toward the door. "Yer Mr. Birmingham is sure to find me out when he sees me table manners. I 'aven't the foggiest which forks to use when."

"Oh, my dearest Dottie," Sophia said with true

remorse, "forgive me for all I've put you through. You've managed very well, and I'm exceedingly proud of you. Don't worry at the table. Just watch me and do as I do."

She started for the door, then stopped and turned back to address her maid, her eyes flashing with mischief. "Could there be another reason you wish to eat with the upper servants? Could you be smitten with Mr. Birmingham's valet?"

"Mr. Thompson can leave his shoes under my bed any night."

Sophia giggled, and then her heart began to flutter at the notion of Mr. Thompson's employer leaving *his* shoes beneath her bed.

"Oh, milady! The back of yer 'air do look like a rat's nest. Are ye sure ye don't want to sit down at the dressing table and let me arrange it for ye?"

Of course she wanted to, especially to render herself more attractive to her dazzling host, but she could not chance one of his servants wandering into the chamber and discovering Dottie's true identity. "Though my hair may not be up to your exacting standards, I seriously doubt it resembles a rodent's nest. You, my dearest Dottie, are possessed of a propensity to exaggerate."

But as Sophia reached the bottom of the stairs and caught a sideways glimpse of her hair in the gilded Adam mirror, she realized with horror that Dottie had not exaggerated.

$\mathcal{C}$hapter 4

Sophia actually availed herself of two feasts that night at dinner. Since she had not eaten since the morning's toast, the food was most welcome. But even more welcome was the vision of Mr. Birmingham seated at the head of the table impeccably dressed in black with crisp white shirt and cravat. Though his manner was courteous, there was a seriousness about him that had not been in his demeanor earlier.

That seriousness was directed at her. Every time she looked up, he was staring at her. As she sipped her soup, she felt his eyes upon her. When she cut her sturgeon, he watched. At the lifting of her wine glass, their eyes met. And held for a moment. Watching him bring the wine glass to his lips caused her to wonder what it would be like to feel those lips upon hers. Nothing like Finkie and his kippers, she was certain.

This Supreme Creature had the most maddening effect upon her. Usually a lively conversationalist, she could do nothing but answer his queries in monosyllables. He was sure to think her an idiot.

As the footmen removed the cloth and brought out the sweetmeats, she decided she really must convince him that she was not going to turn mute like her sister. Unsteady hands folded in her lap, she turned to him and bestowed one of her alluring (so she had often been told) smiles upon him.

The green in his eyes sparkled like shimmering seas.

Then she completely embarrassed herself over the stupidity of her question. "Tell me, Mr. Birmingham, is your father a wealthy man, or did he earn his money?"

"Both, actually. He was born quite poor but was clever about *earning* money. He is dead."

"Was he a . . . gentleman?"

His expression went cold. "No, he was not. It was his fondest wish that his children be groomed to take places in society that were denied him."

Until this moment she had never seen a more confident man than Mr. Birmingham. Her memory flashed back to that morning's dangerous confrontation, to the way Mr. Birmingham had easily bested the armed man who had several advantages over him, not the least of which was his loaded weapon. With deep admiration, she remembered the cocky way Mr. Birmingham had refused her assistance.

Even his home bespoke a man of easy elegance and fine breeding.

Yet she had discovered the one area where he lacked confidence. Handsome, wealthy, gentlemanly Mr. Birmingham was embarrassed over his origins.

In all aspects save one — his mysterious illegal activities — Mr. Birmingham had certainly fulfilled his father's hopes.

As she had done at every dinner since she'd left the school room, Sophia unconsciously slipped into French. "Were your father alive, I believe he would be proud of the man you've become."

Mr. Birmingham laughed. "And I believe you confuse gratitude with admiration."

"I cannot deny that I'm profoundly grateful that you risked your life to save mine this morning, but I assure you my admiration is based on a solid foundation of noble — and gentlemanly — actions on your part."

It only then occurred to her that her host had spoken to her in flawless French. He had most definitely been brought up as a gentleman. "Tell me, Mr. Birmingham, did your father speak French?"

He went serious again. "He spoke nothing except English. And *not* the king's English."

"And you, Mr. Birmingham? What other languages do you speak?"

"German. Italian. Greek. Spanish."

Six languages, counting the English and French he spoke so very well. A most educated man. "And I would guess that you also read and write Latin."

"I had no choice. I began studying with the best tutors my father could buy when I was but four years of age. I was the baby of the family, and by the time I arrived, my father was a very wealthy man."

Sweet meats finished, he stood. "Will you ladies join me in the drawing room? Perhaps we could play loo."

Which was the only game Sophia could think of that three could play. "My sister would prefer to embroider, but I would be most happy to engage in a game of whist with you."

Just one game, then she must become sick. Though she had planned to begin feigning illness at the dining table, she was not yet ready to absent herself from Mr. Birmingham's charming presence.

* * *

He had not intended to spend the night at home. Diane expected him at the theatre after her performance. He always came to her when he returned to London. To her and the exceedingly expensive house he'd set her up in on Park Lane. But Diane was not the woman he wanted to spend this evening with.

Only the ravishing Isadore claimed his attention. His earlier efforts to pen some letters had been fruitless. He could do nothing but think about Isadore. It was not just her formidable beauty that captured his interest — though gazing at her was as pleasurable as breaking the bank at faro. He could think of only one activity that could give more pleasure. And he had given her his word he would not do that.

For what seemed like the hundredth time, William wondered why a woman of such exceptional breeding would be associating herself with smugglers. For he had no doubts this woman was born to the Quality. She spoke court French. She wore expensive clothing of the latest fashion. And — judging from the disarray of her hair — she obviously was used to having her own maid. What could have compelled her to leave her privileged home and court such danger? Money, certainly. But a woman as lovely as Isadore could no doubt snare a royal duke and never have to worry about debts again.

He wished like the devil that sister of hers was not sitting three feet away, an embroidery hoop in her lap. Made it deuced difficult to bring up the topic of gold bullion.

Directly across the game table from him, Isadore was even more beautiful than she'd been at dinner. From the front, her lustrous dark hair swept elegantly from her alabaster face, hiding the unmanageable clumps in the back. She wore a stunning scarlet gown which draped off her bare, white shoulders and barely covered her delectable breasts. A square-cut ruby centered a double strand of pearls clasped at her graceful neck, a neck that begged to be kissed.

He cursed himself for offering that blasted promise.

Since he felt certain he could beat her at whist blindfolded, he quickly arranged the pasteboards in his hands, then lazily perused her. Her slender fingers arranged the cards. Her long, dark lashes lowered. Her snowy white teeth nibbled at her luscious lips. Did the woman have any idea how seductive was her every move?

"Your accommodations are satisfactory?" he asked. Not an especially clever opening, but at least it was better than resorting to the wretched weather.

Those luxurious lashes of hers lifted, and she bestowed upon him a brilliant smile. "Yes, very. The person you employed to decorate the room has taste identical to my own."

"Actually I designed it."

She gave him an incredulous look.

"I travel a good deal—"

"Because of your facility with languages?"

"Yes. That is most helpful in my business dealings."

"And when you travel, you purchase paintings, porcelains, and fine silks for your home?"

He nodded. "In fact, I have an entire warehouse

filled with Grecian and Roman statuary for a country house should I ever settle down long enough to build one."

Her gaze returned to the pasteboards. Was she afraid he would ask questions about her, questions she did not wish to answer?

They played in silence for a few moments before she turned to her sister. "Are you cold, dearest? If you are, we could ask Thompson to bring your shawl."

The much-older sister had to be cold, he thought. No meat at all on those bones of hers.

Miss Dorothea Door's face brightened and she nodded.

He rang for a servant, and when a footman appeared, he requested that Thompson procure the lady's shawl. William's gaze skimmed to Isadore. "What colour is your sister's shawl?"

"Black."

Though Miss Dorothea Door was considerably older than her sibling, it was the younger sister who took the role of a protective older sister, which William found admirable. Her concern for her afflicted must explain her reluctance to leave her sister behind even when Isadore participated in illegal activities.

Thompson soon entered the room and came to present the elder Miss Door her shawl. The sharp features of her face softened when she looked up at his man. It was the most animated he had ever seen the poor creature.

"Allow me to assist you, miss," Thompson said to the plain thing.

Her lashes fluttered as she sat up straighter while Thompson draped the shawl over her bony shoulders.

The unfortunate sister, if William was not mistaken, was thrilled to be the recipient of attentions from Thompson. A pity nothing could come of it. Thompson would never cross that line between upstairs and downstairs. He was far too cognizant of his station.

William barely managed to win the hand, but his satisfaction was short lived. Isadore tossed aside her cards and sank her head into her hands. He leaped to his feet, moving to her. "What's wrong?" He gripped two smooth shoulders and drew in the rose scent of her.

"I don't know what's come over me," she said in a suddenly thin voice. "I'm dreadfully dizzy, and I've a beast of a headache."

"I'll send for a physician."

She shook her head. "I daresay it's nothing more than exhaustion from the tedious journey."

"I pray you haven't taken a chill from the nasty weather."

"I *am* decidedly susceptible to chills," she said in a hoarse whisper, shooting a glance at her sister, whose nod confirmed.

He should not have insisted they come to London today in the near-freezing chill in wet clothing. It would serve him right if she took her death of cold. Anyone could see how delicate she was. He bent to put an arm around her. "Allow me to help you to your chamber."

When they reached the center hall, he instructed the footman to have warm milk sent up to Miss Door's room. "My mother swears that warm milk wards off the worst chills," he told Isadore.

A wan smile on her lips, she went limp against him, her head pillowing on his shoulder. As his arm came around her, he realized how truly small she was. By the constant comparison to her skinny sister, he had thought Isadore voluptuous — perhaps because of her nicely rounded breasts. But now he realized she was every bit as thin as her sister. Only with curves in the appropriate places — places he would not allow himself to contemplate. Not while the poor woman was so sick.

Miss Dorothea Door ran ahead to light a candle and throw back the covers of her sister's bed while William assisted Isadore. Fearing she was too weak to climb upon the bed, William lifted her in his arms then set her down on the smooth white linen. His brows lowered with concern. "I'd feel much more at ease if you would allow me to summon a physician."

She settled a graceful hand on his. "You're very kind, but I daresay a good night's sleep will do me wonders." She turned to her sister. "Will it not, Dorothea?"

The mute nodded.

"Give me your word you will send for me if your condition worsens during the night," he said.

She fell back into the pillows and nodded. "If the need should arise, I'll send my sister to pound upon your door."

"My chambers are directly across the corridor from you."

He fought the urge to bend down and kiss her brow as his mother had done to him when he was sick as a youngster.

Across the corridor in his bedchamber, he settled at his desk to pen those letters left unfinished that afternoon. The room seemed permeated with the scent of roses. Isadore's scent.

Even though it was not yet nine o'clock, William knew he would not see Diane later that night.

Isadore might need him.

* * *

She listened as his footsteps disappeared into his bedchamber. Then she undressed and, with assistance from Dottie, put on her night shift. She stood before the fire, hugging her bare arms and thinking about William Birmingham. Soon, a tear meandered along her cheek.

Dottie rushed to her. "Oh, milady! Whatever is wrong? You truly are sick!"

"I'm cursed, Dottie. Completely cursed. Why could I not have met the Paragon before I made the disastrous decision to wed Lord Finkel?"

"I don't know what a paragon is, milady, but I perceive yer speaking of Mr. Birmingham."

Sophia sniffed. "Indeed I am. He's everything I looked for in the seven and forty men I rejected. He's so. . . magnificent."

Dottie put hands to hips. "Ye said yerself he could be a highwayman."

Sophia glared at her. "And you countered by saying you were convinced he was a gentleman. A very wealthy, fine gentleman. And, you must own, you're always right about people."

Though reason told her Mr. Birmingham made vast amounts of money on the wrong side of the law, her heart told her he was a good man. A gentleman. She collapsed onto her bed, initiating a fresh torrent of tears. "Why did I not listen to you when you warned me about Finkie?"

A knock sounded at the door, and Dottie opened it to take the warm milk. "I'm sure Mr. Birmingham's right about warm milk," Dottie said as she brought the glass to her mistress. "Drink it up, milady, and ye will feel better."

"But I'm *not* taking a chill."

"It'll still make ye feel better."

"Nothing will ever make me feel better. Lord Finkel will never let me go. I feel it in my bones. And I most decidedly do not like the man. I don't want to spend the rest of my life as Lady Finkel."

That, of course, was exactly as Lady Wapping had once felt. But after the evil Lord Wapping took her hefty dowry and subjected the lovely creature to what were said to be unspeakable acts, not even her father or the courts of England could extricate her from the miserable marriage. Under English law, a woman was the property of her husband no matter how vile that husband was.

Dottie, dear soul, refrained from saying `I told you so.' A few minutes later, after she herself had dressed for bed, the maid announced she had a plan to rid her mistress of the unwanted husband.

Sophia swung around to face the maid, her dark eyes glittering.

"Ye must allow Mr. Birmingham to ruin ye. Surely then Lord Finkel wouldn't want ye back."

"That is the most devilish scheme I've ever heard of!" *Even if it was terribly alluring.* "I doubt Mr. Birmingham would be remotely interested in seducing Isadore. I don't know what he wants from the odious woman, but it certainly isn't . . . that bedchamber business. You heard him vow to be a gentleman, and I know he's a noble man incapable of breaking a vow."

"I've seen the way he looks at ye."

Sophia bolted up. "What way?"

"With desire. Sexual desire."

She dared not ask how Dottie knew about

things like sexual desire. A tingling infused her body as she contemplated what her maid had just told her. "While I'll admit you're always right about men, this once you must be mistaken."

Dottie shook her head. "I know what I see."

"You're a pea goose. Blow out the candle and come to bed."

As Sophia lay in the darkness, soft rain falling on the casements, she wondered what it would be like to lie with Mr. Birmingham. The very notion did strange things to her body.

And robbed her of sleep.

* * *

The following morning Mr. Birmingham delivered her breakfast tray himself. Freshly shaven and cheerful, he at least must have had a good night's sleep. Unlike her.

"How are you feeling this morning?" he asked.

"Better, but my head feels as if a regiment of grenadiers danced upon it throughout the night."

His gaze raked over her, sifting down to the white lace robe she had just donned. "I've brought something to help with that. Thompson has a wonderful concoction that works wonders for a bad head."

She had to remember to speak as if it were a great effort. "Then I pray that it helps," she said in a barely audible whisper.

He situated the tray to span her lap, then stood back and directed his comments to Dottie. "I'll stay with your sister for a spell if you have other matters to see to. You cannot have rested well last night."

Sophia could not be left alone with him. He would be sure to ask "Isadore" something that Sophia could not possibly answer. She stiffened.

"No!"

A quizzing look on his face, he spun around to face Sophia.

She lowered her voice. "It's just that my sister worries excessively whenever I am ill. She positively won't let me out of her sight." She lowered her voice even more. "Residual effects from Dorcus's tragic death, no doubt."

He shot Dottie a kindly glance.

"Besides," Sophia added, "as a maiden, I cannot possibly entertain you in my bedchamber."

His eyes went hard. "Then you don't trust me?"

She shrugged. "Actually, I do. I believe you are a gentleman."

"Then since your sister is unable to read to you, allow me. It will help pass the time, take your mind off your discomfort."

How flattered she was that he would devote himself to her when so many other matters must have a claim upon him after his absence from the city. And how incapable she was of allowing him to walk away when she wanted nothing but to spend every minute with him. "Poetry answers very well for my blue devils."

He offered her a lazy smile. "Have you a request?"

"Cowper or Blake. I like them both very much."

He raised his brow. "What, no deathbed stanzas? I thought all ladies were enamored of poems that can only be read with handkerchief in hand."

She shot him an amused gaze. "Oh, I adore that kind of poem," she lied, "but I assumed a gentleman like yourself would not have such in his library."

"I don't." He excused himself to go to his

library.

* * *

He was more convinced than ever that Isadore was a well-born lady. Instead of the insipid, flowery love poems of third-rate poets embraced by women of society's lower rungs, Miss Isadore Door had superb taste in poetry, as in everything else. Save her penchant for embroiling herself in danger.

It occurred to him while he was perusing the volumes of Blake and Cowper and Pope that he and Isadore had a great deal in common. If she had added Pope's name to her list of favored poets, it would surely have been a sign from the Almighty that this woman was his fate. Even if she was a shady lady.

The moment he reentered her bedchamber and beheld her considerable beauty, he grew angry that she was endangering that lovely, lovely neck of hers. By God, he would not have it! He would make her turn straight, even if he had to *give* her, gulp, eighty thousands pounds from his own pocket.

"I brought Cowper," he informed her.

Her only response was a flutter of her lashes and a faint smile.

He brought a chair to her bedside. "Do you have a favorite?" he asked, opening the book.

"You select."

He began to read from *The Winter Evening*. She smiled at his selection, and though it was a long poem, she mouthed along with him several lines.

And when he finished, she said, "This Sylvan Maid thanks you deeply."

Good lord! Sylvan Maid was from an obscure line in Pope's *Windsor Forest*.

She must be The One.
Even if she was a shady lady.

Chapter 5

As thoroughly as she had enjoyed sharing her morning with Mr. Birmingham, whom she kept thinking of as Mr. Perfect (except for the problem with him likely being a criminal), she'd been impatient for him to leave. She simply had to speak to her brother about the difficulty with Finkie.

Devere would know if she had any hope of dissolving the disastrous marriage. They must try to find a way to see that her . . . ahem, *husband* did not get his hands on her dowry.

Though if he would relinquish all claims of being her husband, she would gladly allow him to keep the money. Of course, Devere might have something to say about that.

Her chest tightened when she considered that she would have to tell her brother the manner in which Finkie had compelled her to marry him. That would mean disclosing their sister's dark secret. She had thought never to tell another, but Devere *was* now head of their family. He needed to know. If only she had told him earlier. Before she united herself to Finkie. Before she knew Finkie was not the affable man she had thought him.

As surely as she knew Finkie had sent his servants to the inn at Shelton both the night of her flight and on the next morning, she knew that men in the employ of Lord Finkel would be watching her brother's house. She could not go there.

She would have to send Dottie. Would they also recognize the maid as they had recognized her hooded mistress the previous morning?

Perhaps if she could persuade Mr. Birmingham's valet to escort Dottie there, it would look as if they were a couple calling upon Lord Devere. The valet had always seemed so solicitous of Dottie. The man must be possessed of a tender heart, especially toward a frail female with so limiting an affliction.

She first sketched out her plan to Dottie. "You must bring my brother to me. He's *not to* come in his crested coach, and no one is to know he's my brother. You're to make certain no one follows you here. Then once Devere's here, you're to watch out for Mr. Birmingham's return. I can't allow him to see Devere." It was entirely possible that her brother might be known to Mr. Birmingham, and she couldn't allow Mr. Birmingham to learn she was not Isadore.

Dottie's eyes brightened. "Thompson's to escort me?"

"Yes, I wish for you and the valet to contrive to appear as a well-born couple."

"Yer brother's apt to give me away in front of Mr. Thompson."

"We can't have that. I'll scribble a note to him, telling him *not* to acknowledge a previous acquaintance with you. And I'll explain that it's important you play the role of a mute. A high-born mute." Sophia drew a deep breath. "I'll also tell him I'm in danger."

There was a whimsical look on Dottie's smiling face.

"Why in the devil are you smiling about me being in danger?" Sophia demanded.

"I ain't smiling because yer in danger—which I won't deny. I'm smiling because I get to spend the afternoon pretending to be a couple with 'andsome Mr. Thompson."

Sophia's eyes narrowed. "Give me your word that you'll not slip and speak to Thompson."

Dottie sighed. "Very well, milady."

Sophia then summoned a servant and asked that servant to summon Mr. Birmingham's valet. While she waited, she penned a letter to Devere.

My dear brother,

I am in grave danger and need you to come to me. I've sent Dottie to fetch you because your house is almost certainly being watched by servants of the vile Lord Finkel. Pray, do NOT acknowledge Dottie. It's imperative that she's thought to be my mute sister. Come to me at Grosvenor Square—but not in a vehicle with your crest. And make sure you're not being followed.-Sophia

When Thompson arrived at the sitting room off Sophia's bedchamber, she said, "I hope your master will not object if I ask your assistance this afternoon." She eyed him in an attempt to determine if he could pass as gentry or possibly even nobility.

His austere clothing—a black cutaway coat over a white shirt paired with black trousers—was as immaculate and tasteful as his master's. But it needed brightening.

As she peered at him, she was reminded of Dottie's fierce attraction to the man. It was an attraction Sophia failed to understand. The valet was at least a decade older than his master and several inches taller. Master and servant were quite a contrast. Mr. Birmingham was just under six feet and burly with golden hair. Mr. Thompson was over six foot, lean, and possessed of straight black hair. She supposed his face was nice enough.

Thompson nodded. "Mr. Birmingham has charged me with looking after you sisters."

"Since I'm not altogether well, I need to send my sister to carry out a commission for me, but you must know how difficult it is for her, given her . . . condition."

"I would be honored to be of assistance to your sister."

"I need you to escort her to Curzon Street. It's not very far, but I worry about her."

"I will protect her with my very life."

* * *

Before William went to his brother's on Threadneedle Street, he stopped at London's finest coachmaker's and ordered a new coach. When Isadore's health was restored, he might need to convey her about the city, and he did not want her taking another chill. He felt responsible for her present state of ill health. If only he'd not allowed the ladies to ride all those hours in the rain.

"My current coach has suffered casualties from a band of highwayman." He ignored the coachmaker's exclamations and continued. "I wondered if you could loan me a coach until the new one's made. I'd be most happy to pay a fair price for its rental."

"Certainly, Mr. Birmingham. Allow me to show you one of the used coaches I have for sale."

William made his selection, they came to terms,

and William continued on to The City. Later he would send a servant to bring home the tilbury he'd arrived in at the coachmaker's. As he rode into the City, he chastised himself. What made him think Isadore would still be with him when the new coach was finished? She could exchange the gold bullion with him tomorrow and pass out of his life forever.

He did not like to contemplate that.

When he reached Nick's establishment, he jumped down from the box and tethered his horse. It was late enough in the day to expect Nick here rather than at the Exchange.

When William entered the inner chamber to Nick's office, his elder brother looked up from a ledger he'd been perusing. William was struck by the dissimilarity of the brothers' appearance. No one ever took them for brothers. As it happened, Will was the only one of the four siblings who was not possessed of dark hair and eyes, and he was the only one of the three brothers who was muscular. He sighed. He would have liked to have his brothers' height.

"How was our sister?" Nick asked.

William had almost forgotten that visiting their sister in the North had masked his clandestine purpose of traveling there. "Apparently, breeding suits her. She looked lovely, and Agar treats her as if she's made of eggshells. Doting is not a strong enough word." William dropped into a chair by the fire.

"I cannot in my wildest dreams imagine our meek little sister ever living the role of lady of the manor. She's such a quiet little thing."

"Agar is encouraging her to not be so excessively humble, and I'll say she actually looks as if she's always been Lady Agar. I believe the staff rather worship her for her kindliness and gentle ways."

"I was happy that someone from her own family went to see her. It had to be difficult to be away from her family for the first time in her life."

"Don't worry about Verity. She and Agar are uncommonly happy." He eyed Nick. "Allow me to rephrase. Perhaps not uncommon—given that you and Lady Fiona are equally as nauseatingly in love."

Nick chuckled. "I hope you experience something just as satisfying. You need to stop living out of a portmanteau and settle down with a nice wife. Agar and I highly recommend marriage."

Will was powerless to keep his thoughts from drifting to Isadore. It had fleetingly crossed his mind that she was *THE* one. How could he even think of such a thing about a woman who could likely end up in prison? Or worse. "I believe I'll wait until I'm thirty."

"If you live to be thirty. Is there nothing Adam or I can do to make you abandon your dangerous pursuits? Good God, man, it's not as if you need the money!"

"I'm not cut out to be a banker like Adam or a stockbroker like you. Spending every day at the same place – indoors, at that—would be worse than treading water in the middle of the ocean. I'd die."

"I wish you'd come to the Exchange. I cannot convey how exhilarating it is to win and lose fortunes every day."

"I probably will—after I marry. When others depend upon me I will no longer risk my neck. Then I'll likely risk other people's money—as you do."

Nick laughed. "How was the other part of your journey?"

"I'm getting closer."

Nick raised a brow. "Closer to bringing that vile piece of dung to justice?"

"That . . . or crushing him. I'll get him one way or the other. I keep learning of more innocent lives he's destroyed."

"Yet he dances through Society as a peer beyond reproach." Nick shook his head. "It was a bloody shame about Stoney."

"Perhaps something good will come of his death—if I can expose Lord Finkel's deeds most foul."

"And have you the bullion?"

"Not yet. But MacIver's go-between has made contact with me."

"The mysterious Isadore?"

Will pictured her. Would that a Romney could capture her incredible beauty with those rich dark eyes set in a creamy face and crowned by sparkling brown locks enhanced with glints of red. He nodded, a smile curving his lips.

"Was she as pretty as MacIver said?"

"Prettier."

"When does she give you the bullion?"

"I don't know."

"What do you mean?"

"There are circumstances that have conspired to keep us from communicating about the bullion."

Nick's dark eyes narrowed. "What the hell?"

"There's her mute sister, who I believe is in the dark about Isadore's illegal activities. And there's the armed men who tried to abduct her. Or . . ."

Nick held up a hand. "Armed men?"

"Thompson and I handily dispatched them. The only casualty was my coach."

"You think they thought you had the bullion?"

"Not directly. Somehow they must have known Isadore has access to it because they wanted her."

"Where in the devil is the bullion?"

"I don't know. Isadore's supposed to connect me with it."

"Why can't you just ask her?

"I've not been able to have a private moment with her."

"Then for God's sake, go ahead and ask her in front of the sister. I don't suppose one could hope the sister's also deaf?"

"No, her hearing is normal." William sighed. "I wouldn't feel right being the one to bring up the subject. Isadore's awfully protective of her sister. I shouldn't want to be the source of friction in their family."

"How can you get back in communication with Isadore?"

"She's actually staying at Grosvenor Square with me."

Nick gave him a sly smile. "Is she now? And I'll vow you've enjoyed that very much."

"It's not what you think. She's a . . . lady."

Nick burst out laughing. "Of course. A lady who smuggles gold bullion into the country. A lady who's acquainted with MacIver. You must be losing your touch, old fellow. I always thought you had a good eye for the ladies."

"You can't possibly understand. She's not like you think. . ."

"Are you sure you and she . . . ?"

"The extent of our intimacy was that I read

poetry to her."

A hearty laugh broke from Nick, and soon he began to guffaw. When he was finally able to restore his decorum, he said, "I've got to meet your Isadore."

"She's not *my* Isadore."

"Listen to your older brother. Go home and demand that she tell you where in the bloody hell the bullion is." Nick regarded his brother solemnly for a moment. "I was never in favor of you buying the bullion in such a manner, but once you started, Adam and I have lined up buyers. We can't let them down. I need to know when we can expect delivery."

Nodding ruefully, Will got up and bid his brother farewell.

* * *

Sophia listened patiently as her brother climbed the stairs, but the moment his feet hit the landing, she ran from her chambers and threw herself into his arms. He patted her back in a rather patronizing manner before separating from her and regarding her with a serious expression. "What the bloody hell did you do to Finkel?"

She sighed. "Come, let's speak in private."

"Who's place is this?"

"A wealthy man named William Birmingham."

His brows lowered. "Nicholas Birmingham's brother?"

"Was that the one who married Lord Agar's sister?"

"Yes, and his sister wed Lord Agar."

"That can't be my Mr. Birmingham."

"There's another Birmingham brother who's a banker."

She shook her head. "This man couldn't

possibly be a banker, and I've seen the sinfully handsome Nicholas Birmingham. Believe me, William Birmingham cannot be related to him. Though he's handsome, he's not tall, and he's not dark like Nicholas Birmingham. Can you credit Nicholas Birmingham with a golden-haired brother?"

"Not really." He scanned the opulent surroundings as they strode to her chambers. "What are you doing here with a man who's clearly not your husband?"

She closed the door and bade that he sit beside her on the settee near the fire. "I'm not sure. He thinks I'm a woman named Isadore."

"You've lost me."

"Tell me, have you heard from Lord Finkel?"

"I have, and he's livid. He says you abandoned him on your wedding night, but he insists on forgiving you—which I thought was rather generous of him."

"There's nothing generous about him. I've come to believe he may actually be wicked."

"Why did you marry him if you didn't love him? Don't even *like* him from the sound of it!"

"I had a good reason, though my decision was probably also tempered by the fact I was facing confirmed spinsterhood. I had turned down almost fifty suitors and had come to believe that I would never find a man I could love. No woman wants to be an old maid with no home and family of her own." How she wished she had waited! She now believed there quite possibly *was* a man she could love. Even if he was most likely a dodgy character.

Her eyes solemn, she peered at her brother and continued. "Lord Finkel did something which compelled me to accept his offer. Like you, I was fooled by what I thought of as his generosity."

"How did he compel you?"

She sighed. "I had planned to take Maryann's secret to the grave, but I can no longer do so. We—you and I—must stop Lord Finkel from having the power to destroy an innocent lady."

"Maryann?"

A grave expression on her face, Sophia nodded. "During a stay at the Colgroves' Stonebridge Manor with her friend Lady Louisa, Maryann behaved in an inappropriate and foolish manner with the Colgroves' second-eldest son, whom she'd always been sweet on."

"Dear God, she couldn't have . . ." His brows shot up.

Sophia nodded. "She was only fifteen. He was seventeen and scheduled to go fight in the Peninsula. They were both young, fancied themselves in love, and feared that they might never see each other again once he went off to war."

"And Finkel knew of this . . . intimacy?"

"I don't know how he did. In fact, I didn't believe him. Until I confronted Maryann. She was horrified that anyone else could ever have found out—then she remembered that Lady Louisa had told her someone in Spain had stolen all her brother's letters from his tent. Maryann had written to Captain Landsdowne about her regrets."

"Are you saying that in order to secure your hand in marriage, Finkel threatened to expose our sister—and ruin her chance to ever marry?"

"Yes. I think, too, he wanted more than my hand. Don't forget I had a sizeable dowry."

Devere uttered a curse.

Her brother had never used such words in front of her before. Nor had he ever said bloody hell. Until today. She supposed discussion of Finkie merited foul language. He was proving to be a most foul man.

"I have now decided that since you're head of the family, you must decide how to approach Lord Finkel."

"I'd bloody well want to murder him!"

"That is not an option." She frowned. "Will he be entitled to my dowry?"

Devere cursed again. "I'll put my solicitor on it." He shook his head. "I just keep remembering the case with poor Lady Wapping."

"Me, too. Oh Devere, you must help me. I don't want to be like Lady Wapping."

His hand cupped hers. "I'll speak to my solicitor." He stood. "Come, I'll take you home."

She shook her head. "I can't go there. I know Lord Finkel has to have servants watching Devere House." Her voice cracked. "I believe they would forcibly remove me. They tried to abduct me yesterday, but Mr. Birmingham and his valet— whose not like any valet I've ever heard of— thwarted them."

"How could Finkel's servants be authorized to abduct the lady of the manor?"

"I'm telling you they did. And they were armed. They did not treat me with even a modicum of respect. You'd have thought I was a common criminal the way they spoke and acted with me."

Her brother cursed again. "That is in no way satisfactory." He came back to the settee and squeezed her shoulder. "We've got to find a way to get you out of this. I'm also going to speak with

Finkel, but I don't like leaving you here with this . . . this Birmingham fellow."

"He's a gentleman. I have no fears for my safety or my virtue as long as I'm with him."

"I must at least speak with him."

"I can't have him know who I really am. I am only welcome because he believes I'm Isadore."

"Who is Isadore?"

"I wish I knew."

He strode to the door. "I'll return tomorrow."

"You mustn't come when Mr. Birmingham is here. I'll send a note around when he leaves." She thought for a moment. "If ever you wish to talk to me, look up at my window. If Mr. Birmingham is out, you will see a brace of candles right here." She pointed to the ledge beneath the tall window. "If he's at home, there will be no candelabra."

* * *

"I thought you might be interested to know that Miss Isadore Door had a caller today," Thompson said to William as he was tying his cravat for dinner.

William raised a quizzing brow. "A male caller?"

"Indeed."

"Who was he?"

"I don't know, but I do know that he resides in a fine home on Curzon Street."

"Now how would you know that?"

"Because Miss Isadore Door asked that her sister and I go there. Miss Dorothea Door carried a note to the gentleman who resides there."

"Do you know what the note said?"

The valet shook his head.

"Where did Isadore meet with this gentleman?"

"In your mother's chambers. The sitting room there, I believe."

"And the door was closed?"

"It was."

"It must be the person she's entrusted with the bullion. It's rather odd that a man who lives on a fine street like Curzon would be mixed up with smuggling."

"No odder than a gentleman who lives on Grosvenor Square. And like you, this man was a gentleman." Thompson cleared his throat. "You may wish to know that Miss Isadore Door embraced the man."

William felt as if he'd been kicked in the gut.

What was this so-called gentleman to Isadore? William didn't like to think of her being connected in any way with another man.

Thompson helped him on with his dinner jacket. William was tired of dancing around the issue of the bullion. The time had come to ask Isadore outright. He was going to the dinner table right now.

$\mathcal{C}$hapter 6

By the time he reached the dinner room, his rising anger prevented him from cordially greeting Isadore. The tight control he exercised over his tongue did not extend to his eyes. They raked over the stunning woman in red velvet. Her dark lashes lifted as he neared the table, and a soft smile lifted the corners of her mouth. She was exquisite.

He quickly averted his gaze and addressed the sister. "Good evening, Miss Door." Then he allowed his gaze to skim toward the lovely one. "You must be feeling better, Miss Door."

She sighed. "It's not that I'm actually greatly improved. It's rather that I was possessed of a vast need to leave the confines of my bedchamber."

He was unable to suppress a chuckle as he slid into his chair at the head of the table. "Forgive me if I fail to extend sympathies. You can't have been too bored. I understand you entertained a gentleman caller in your bedchamber today, did you not?" William was certain the man was up to no good.

"Not actually in my bedchamber. I spent the day on the settee in the adjacent sitting room. That's where I spoke to the gentleman."

His eyes were hard when he spoke. "So is he the one who's got our bullion?" There! It was out. No more ambiguity.

She did not respond for a moment. "What

would make you think that, Mr. Birmingham?"

"You must be anxious to conclude our exchange and get back to your . . . home." It suddenly occurred to him that she might have lied to him about being a maiden. Perhaps she was a married woman. Was today's caller her husband?

Why did the idea cause his stomach to roil?

"The way I feel at present, I'm not up to the journey home."

He was not about to express sympathy. "And where would that home be?"

She hesitated before answering. "You must understand that a woman in my position is not at liberty to reveal such details."

"Speaking of *a woman in your position*, you did not answer my question about your gentleman caller."

She shook her head. "He no longer has the bullion."

"But he told you where it is?"

"Certainly. But I cannot tell you where it is at present."

"Not until you receive your eighty thousand guineas."

Her huge dark eyes rounded for a split second. "When can I expect my payment?"

"I have it now."

She turned to her sister and placed a trembling hand on that lady's forearm. "Pray, dearest, I feel a relapse coming on. I know I shouldn't have come down those stairs. It was too much for me." With each spoken word, her voice had faded a little more until her last words were barely audible.

Both ladies rose, the lovely one clinging to the thinner one. Isadore turned to him and spoke in a faint voice. "Forgive me, but I must take my leave.

I fear I may collapse."

He jumped up. "Pray, allow me to assist." With that, he proceeded to pluck her up into his arms as if she were a small child.

Though he was a strong man, by the time he'd mounted two flights of stairs carrying her, he had difficulty catching his breath. The sister opened Isadore's chamber door, and he carried her to the bed and tossed her upon it.

He was not convinced she was truly sick. It almost seemed as if she were pretending to be sick in order to keep from having to produce the bullion. Had she lost it? Sold it to another? No, otherwise she'd not have been awaiting him at the Prickly Pig Inn. But why in the devil did she wish to prolong her stay here at Grosvenor Square?

* * *

Once Sophia was assured that Mr. Birmingham had departed her chamber and returned to the dinner room, her voice was restored with remarkable clarity. "Oh, Dottie, I have so gotten myself into a pickle!"

"I don't call getting eighty thousand guineas a pickle. Sounds like a dream come true to me."

"You forget the eighty thousand is for Isadore."

"But I thought you was Isadore."

"I most certainly am not. You've known me all my life. I'm Sophia Beresford."

Dottie shook her head. "Not no more. Yer Sophia Finkel."

In exaggerated fashion, Sophia closed her eyes and groaned. "Pray, do not remind me."

"At least you now know why he wanted Isadore."

"Yes. For the bullion. It seems the source of our dear Mr. Birmingham's wealth is gold smuggling."

"Leastways he ain't a killer or something truly vile."

"There is that," Sophia said with resignation.

"I think he's getting impatient to get his hands on the bullion."

"I daresay you're right. What am I to do?"

"I don't see why you can't return to Devere House."

"Because I have a strong conviction that Lord Finkel's men will know when I arrive, and their master will force me to return to him. Right now, the law is on his side. Devere would have no choice but to allow Finkie to take me away."

"I can't believe dear Lord Devere would allow that."

"Do you not recall the heartbreaking story of Lady Wapping's disastrous marriage? I was only a child at the time, but it is still being talked about."

Dottie shook her head. "I don't have privy to all the tales of the *ton.*"

Sophia drew a deep breath. "Lady Wapping's beauty had accounted for her vastly successful come-out. She was widely courted, but gave her heart to Lord Wapping." Sophia sighed again. "On the night of her marriage, Lord Wapping—for reasons no one has ever been able to ascertain—beat her soundly. As soon as she could, she stole away back to her parents. Her head was bashed, an arm was broken, and she was bruised all over."

Dottie winced. "They ought to have hung the man!"

"I agree, but no justice was ever served. Lord Wapping went to collect her at her father's. Her father said he would not permit his daughter to return to the beast. Lord Wapping countered by saying the lady was his property, and the laws of

England would uphold his right to get her back. The father said the laws did not apply to men capable of such horrid violence—to which Wapping replied that a husband had the right of punishing a wife who was not compliant."

Dottie's brows lowered. "She didn't want to bed her husband?"

Sophia shrugged. "The lady said she was compliant."

"Then her husband must have been a sex maniac."

"Obviously, he was not normal. The pity of it was that the courts eventually ruled that her husband had the right to take his wife away from her father, and he had the right to beat his wife if he wanted—provided it wasn't excessive. Which I understand to mean as long as he doesn't kill her."

"It must have been powerful hard for her papa to let her return to the beast."

Sophia nodded. "He had to be restrained. But not for long. He killed Lord Wapping rather than allow the fiend to hurt his daughter, and the poor father was hanged for the killing."

Dottie's eyes swelled with tears. "Oh, milady! That could be you! Why did you ever marry that horrid man?"

"I had my reasons." There had to be some other way to save Maryann's reputation. It was such a relief to share her dread with Devere. Surely he could resolve Maryann's problem.

"Is Lord Devere going to see if there's some way he can get ye out of that marriage?"

"He was to go directly to his solicitor when he left here." She kept thinking about Lady Wapping.

"I do hope yer brother will succeed."

"As if this difficulty with my . . . *marriage* wasn't horrid enough, now I've gotten myself involved in smuggling gold."

"Not you. Isadore."

Sophia glowered at her maid.

Dottie sighed. "Whatever will you do?"

"I have no idea. That's why I had to pretend I was gravely ill. I had to get away from Mr. Birmingham and form a plan." She eyed her maid. "You know how beastly inept I am at thinking on the fly."

"The fact is, milady, you're beastly inept at choosing husbands too!"

"You needn't remind me. I regret it every second of the day."

Dottie screwed up her face in thought. "I don't suppose ye've got any gold bullion?"

Sophia scowled. "What do you think?"

"I guess that would be the real Isadore. A pity you can't find her."

"Hmmm. That's actually a very good idea, Dottie."

"But ye can't find her if yer laid up like an invalid."

"True. But . . . it's now obvious to me that Mr. Birmingham had been told that a woman named Isadore who possessed the bullion would be contacting him. That would explain why when I approached him at the Prickly Pig Inn he immediately thought I was Isadore. I believe that Mr. Birmingham might also have thought that thieves interested in the gold—and not Finkie's hired hands—were the men trying to abduct me the following morning."

Dottie nodded.

"So it stands to reason the real Isadore will be

trying to make contact with Mr. Birmingham."

"She could come knocking upon his door this very minute!"

"A very good point! Thank goodness my chamber faces Grosvenor Square. I'll just push my settee up to the window and keep a vigil. It's imperative I intercept her before she speaks to Mr. Birmingham."

"If you could get the eighty thousand from Mr. Birmingham, you could buy the bullion from her."

"Exactly!"

"But how long must you pretend to be dreadful sick?"

"As long as it takes."

"I know how much you hate staying indoors, how much you thrive on being around all yer friends and family."

"I will own, it is most difficult."

Dottie eyed her askance. "Did it seem to you that Mr. Birmingham was a bit out of charity with you tonight?"

"Indeed, it did."

"I'd wager he's angry because you 'ad a gentleman caller. Jealous, he is, mark me words."

"But the gentleman caller was my brother!"

"Mr. Birmingham don't know that!"

"I'm sure he wouldn't be jealous. It's not as if he's ever given me the slightest indication that he's interested in me in that way."

"In the way yer interested in him?"

Sophia nodded ruefully.

"You said you would listen to Dottie after yer fiasco with Lord Finkel. I'm always right about men."

"Oh, Dottie, how I wish you could be right about this!"

"I'll say it again. I can see how you feel about the 'andsome Mr. Birmingham. I say you ought to let him ruin you. Surely Lord Finkel wouldn't want spoiled goods."

"I wouldn't have any idea how one would go about getting ruined, how I could possibly seduce the handsome gentleman." There was great merit in what Dottie suggested. Meeting Mr. Birmingham had a remarkable effect upon her. Almost overnight she'd gone from disliking a man's kisses to hungering for a certain man's kisses—and more.

"Why don't ye get yerself all pretty, and I'll take a note to Mr. Birmingham begging that he come read to me melancholy sister? That should mellow him. Ye know how gentle like he was with you last night."

"I can't write such a note. I'd look like a strumpet!"

"But I can write it, saying as how concerned I am for me sister."

Sophia heaved a huge sigh. "First could you return to the dinner room? I cannot tell you how hungry I am. I should like you to bring me something."

"Leave it to Dottie."

* * *

His plans to see Diane tonight were abandoned as soon as the poor mute delivered him her scribbled letter, urging him to come read to her melancholy sister. As out of charity as he was with Isadore, he was powerless to resist jumping to her every whim.

It was he—and not her sister—who carried the supposedly infirm lady a plate of food. He softly knocked upon her door, and when he entered, he nearly lost his breath at the sight of her semi-reclining on the settee, a vision in frothy white lace. Her pretty face brightened when she looked up and saw him.

He was not unaffected by her. Much to his chagrin.

"You must be hungry," he said, his voice tender. "I've brought you some food your sister picked out."

She sat up straighter and spoke in a feeble voice. "It probably would do me good to eat. I feel so very weak."

He set the plate on the tea table near her settee.

She took the fork he'd brought, stabbed at the veal, and ate it most appreciatively. "I confess, I was hungry. How very kind of you to bring this to me. Pray, won't you take a seat?"

He sat next to her on the settee.

"Where is my sister?"

"She was apparently very hungry. I don't think I've ever seen so thin a person stack a plate so very high with food. I would be surprised if she cleaned the plate in under a half hour."

Isadore giggled. "My sister is possessed of a hearty appetite." Then the lady launched into a coughing fit. It was more an asthmatic cough than one productive of mucus or—heaven forbid, the spitting of blood associated with consumption.

When she finished coughing, her attention returned to her plate. It seemed the two sisters shared a healthy appetite. He was unable to remove his gaze from her loveliness. She was just as pretty in profile as she was from the front. He tried to analyze just what it was about her that was so beautiful. She was in possession of dark lashes that were impossibly long, but there were so many more components to her beauty. In the firelight, her skin looked as smooth and fair as polished ivory. Her nose was perfection, as was her graceful neck. His gaze moved to the sweet swell of her bosom, and he drew in his breath. Then averted his gaze.

He wished to God he hadn't given his word not to seduce her. He'd never wanted to kiss anyone as he wanted to kiss Isadore at this moment.

He went to the table in her room where a decanter of port reposed, and he poured each of them a glass. When she finished eating, she took up her glass, then turned her full attention to him. Their eyes met and held. Even though hers were nearly as dark as coal, they were uncommonly expressive. Solemn.

She clinked her glass to his. "To a successful completion to our partnership."

She drank. He drank. Few words passed between them. Soon he was bringing the whole bottle to the tea table, and they drank every last drop of it.

He wondered if she was not accustomed to spirits, for it had such a mellowing effect upon her. She began to stroke the planes of his face whilst speaking tenderly. "I do believe I owe my life to you, my dear Mr. Birmingham."

His ability to remain a perfect gentleman began to wane. He found himself lifting her hand and pressing soft lips into her palm. He grew excited by the sharp intake of her breath. Then, if he wasn't mistaken, she began to purr almost like a feline. She settled her head upon his shoulder, and his arm came around her.

"I am regretting that ridiculous promise I made

to you," he said, his voice husky.

Her head came off his shoulders, her eyes fixed on his. "About not trying to seduce me?"

"That too, but right now I'm longing to kiss you."

* * *

It was as if her heart exploded. His words shattered any self control she had possessed. She inched closer to him, so close that she could feel his breath and smell his sandalwood scent. For the first time in her seven-and-twenty years, she found herself lifting her face to welcome a man's kiss.

But this was not just any man. This was the man she'd been seeking for the past decade and had come to believe did not exist. But exist he did. She could weep for the want of him.

Their lips came together with urgency. Neither of them could control this raging need to touch, to taste, to feel possessed. She stiffened when their mouths opened to one another, but any resistance was short lived beneath the intoxicating pleasure of this magical blending. What repulsed with any other man thrilled when initiated by . . . *William.* William Birmingham. His very name accelerated her pulse.

She did not want the kiss to ever end. Her fuzzy, spiraling thoughts had her envisioning William climbing inside her. She was overcome with a need to feel him inside of her.

He began to trace a trail of wet kisses along the column of her neck, to the gap where her lace dressing gown came together. He flicked the lace aside to reveal her bare breasts.

He groaned, and she became even more aroused. When his mouth closed over a nipple, she was certain the very breath had been sucked from her. Her lower torso began to squirm, then to pulse toward him.

He suddenly drew away, his gaze lovingly lingering on her exposed breasts as he tenderly recovered them with the lace dressing gown. "Forgive me," he said in a throaty voice. "I got carried away. I forgot you were ill."

She felt like one drugged on laudanum. "I have a confession."

His green eyes shimmered with mirth. "You're not really ill?"

She nodded. "I would have said or done anything that would ensure I could stay here with you." Her hand cupped his cheek again. "From the moment you came into my life I . . . have been strongly attracted to you."

He sighed. "You aren't making this easy for me, Isadore. I cannot convey to you how badly I want to make love to you, but I did give you my word."

"I absolve you of making any false promises."

He kissed her cheek. "It's not that easy. There's the fact you're a maiden. I don't fancy debauching an innocent."

"Even if that *innocent* wants you to more than she's ever wanted anything?" Her voice had gone faint again.

* * *

As he wanted her. More than he'd ever wanted any woman. When she'd told him of her attraction, he'd felt an elation like nothing he'd ever known. He felt as if he could leap over Westminster Abbey.

His own attraction to her was so much more than this aching, physical need. Her beauty, her intelligence, her compassion for her afflicted sister, her taste in poetry, all these attributes elevated her far above all the women he'd ever known.

And now this supreme sexual compatibility. *She's THE one.*

He went to heave a sigh, but he was so aroused, his sigh sputtered. Then he hauled her into his arms and greedily kissed her.

"Then, my dearest Isadore, I hope you'll never regret this night of lovemaking."

$\mathcal{C}$hapter 7

When she awakened the following morning, a deep sense of well-being suffused her. A bird's chirp outside her window seemed to reverberate into her very soul, as if her heart were singing. Last night had been the most wonderful night of her life. William was her destiny.

For some odd reason, one of her first thoughts upon awakening was that surely Finkie wouldn't want her now—now that she'd allowed another man access to every part of her body. As many times as she had eagerly taken in William's seed the previous night, she could even be carrying his babe. Surely Finkie would be so repelled over such a prospect he would be happy to dissolve their so-called marriage.

She rolled to her side to avail herself of a view of the supremely handsome man to whom she'd given her heart—and so much more. His eyes were open. He'd been watching her. His golden good looks were just as appealing in the light of day as they'd been beneath candlelight. She could never tire of gazing at that sun-burnished skin, or of his golden locks, or muscular physique. Her gaze trailed to the curly blond hairs on his chest, and she scooted closer so she could pillow her head there.

His arms came around her as he pressed kisses into her hair. "You know we must marry."

Words that should have made her the happiest woman in all God's earth instead felt like a hot meteor had torn through her.

For a few moments she thought about telling him the truth about her identity, about her sham marriage. But she knew the only thing he would hear would be that she belonged to another man. She must wait to see if there was anything her brother could do to terminate her marriage. Was there any hope?

"I should never wish to marry a man who felt compelled to ask for my hand."

"But Isadore, my love, you and I both know there's an undeniable force compelling us to be with one another. Always."

She could weep. He hadn't exactly said he loved her, but what he said was close. He wasn't offering marriage because he'd taken the virginity she'd so needily offered. He was offering marriage because he knew what she knew: they belonged together. Oh, yes, she could cry a river.

Her eyes moist, she lifted her head to kiss his cheek. Then, clutching the sheet to her, she climbed down off the big four-poster bed. "I shall certainly consider your offer, my dear Mr. Birmingham."

He sat up in bed and eyed her with hostility. Since she had pulled off the sheet, he was naked, gloriously naked. "Don't call me *Mister* Birmingham."

Her voice softened. "Yes, William." How she wanted to say, "My love," but she could not do so until she was free.

He too hopped off the bed and stepped into the breeches he'd thrown off in a heated frenzy the night before. She slipped back into her lace wrapper. He came to take her in his arms and drop kisses onto her neck.

She could go mad with want of this man. "I suppose everyone in your house—including my sister—knows I'm ruined."

"My servants are discreet. I thought perhaps your sister was encouraging our . . . union."

"She likely did. Ever since the night at the inn, she's been singing your praises—via notes." Sophia turned and pressed against him. "She thinks you are perfect for me."

He lifted her chin. "How many proposals of marriage have you turned down?"

"If I tell you, you'll think I'm a terrible flirt."

"You're not a flirt. How many, Isadore? Fifteen?"

"More."

"Twenty?"

"It's so embarrassing. I've received seven-and-forty proposals, but I kept waiting for the man who would ignite a passion in me." She peered up. "I've been waiting for you, William."

"And I was *not* looking for a wife, but then I knew two nights ago—because of the Pope reference—you were *THE* one."

Her eyes widened, her mouth opened. A dreamy look washed across her face. Moments passed before she could speak. "You admire Pope too?"

"Greatly." He drew away. "I cannot be this close to you and not wish to carry you back to that bed, but I cannot. I have a meeting at noon."

"Then you'd best go shave and make yourself look refreshed. I can't say that I'm at all sorry I caused you to lose sleep last night."

* * *

William had scheduled a meeting with MacIver

for the purpose of learning everything he could about Isadore. The woman had totally bewitched him.

They met at a coffee house on the Strand. It was place where the day's newspapers were passed around so that men could keep informed without having to pay the hefty subscription fees. MacIver was one of the scruffiest-looking men in the establishment. Frankly, William was surprised he'd chosen this location because MacIver didn't seem the type who wanted to read about public affairs.

William slid into a chair in front of the tiny round table MacIver had claimed for them.

"What's up, guv'nah?"

"I need to know everything you can tell me about Isadore."

"She ain't contacted you yet?"

"Yes, she has."

MacIver's blue eyes regarded him intensely for a moment. "I was surprised when she told me she'd never met you."

"Why?" William asked.

"Because she's so much like you. She travels throughout the continent, speaks several languages, and takes many foolish risks with her beautiful neck."

"Then I am surprised our paths haven't crossed. She's usually dealing with gold bullion?"

"Not necessarily. Sometimes she is actually the compliant wife to her upstanding husband."

William felt as if a cannon ball had just torn through his chest. "Husband? Then she's . . . married?" His thoughts flitted to the previous night and the pleasure she'd given him. He would have wagered the entire Birmingham fortune that she'd never before been with a man.

"Yes. She doesn't fancy her *business* associates knowing her true identity because her husband is not only ignorant of her clandestine activities, but he's also in a lofty position for the Foreign Office."

William swallowed over the huge lump in his throat. "Would I know him?"

"If you've not had dealings with him, you'd know him. The British ambassador to the Hague."

"Dear God. Lord Evers!" William had not only met him. He was very fond of the congenial fellow. He knew, too, that when Evers inherited, all he'd received was the title. No money.

Apparently, Isadore was rectifying that.

MacIver nodded. "I beg that you keep the lady's *activities* to yourself. It wouldn't do for Lord Evers to learn by what means his wife has added to the family fortune."

William was reeling from the discovery that *his* Isadore belonged to another. He felt as if he were falling from a mighty tree.

MacIver continued to regard him with all-knowing eyes. "I can see ye've fallen under her spell. Yer not the first. She's never allowed marriage to keep her from her little romantic *flirtations*. Ye know how women of the *ton* are."

William wanted to crash a fist into the man's face for saying these things about Isadore. He couldn't be speaking of Isadore. She wasn't like that! Anger surged through him. He gulped down his coffee, got to his feet, threw a crown on the table, and stormed from the shop without saying farewell to his long-time associate.

Since he'd ridden his horse here, he felt like a bruising ride. He went to Hyde Park and galloped over the bridal paths as if a raging ball of fire was chasing him. He wasn't sure that raging ball of fire wasn't burning through him right now.

Many women, many beautiful women had passed through his life in the nine years since he left university, but none of them had ever affected him as Isadore. When they were together last night, bare skin to bare skin, they were as one. She had possessed him like warm honey flowing into every cell in his body.

A deep and gnawing anger ate through him. He'd never experienced a blacker day than this, this day that had begun with his offer of marriage. His first. He'd been filled with joy this morning. And now there was only bleak hopelessness.

For more than an hour, he rode as fast and as hard as he could. Then the sky turned dark. At first there were sprinkles. Then the skies erupted. He ought to return to Grosvenor Square. But that's where *she* was. He didn't know how he could bear seeing her and knowing she belonged to another.

He wasn't even certain he could contain his fury.

Of course, he didn't have to have intercourse with her.

All the way back to his home he wondered what he should say. She had made it clear last night she had no wish to go to her home. God! Now that he remembered her words, *A woman in my position cannot reveal too much.* They made perfect sense in the light of what he now knew about her and her respectable husband. Was Lord Evers even in London? Why in the devil did she not want to go to her husband?

After last night, William believed in his soul it was he whom she wanted. But, of course, that could never be. For one thing, he respected Lord Evers far too much.

He wondered if she would ever be honest with him.

Before he reached Grosvenor Square he had come to some decisions. He would avoid her, except when they made the bullion exchange. If she still wanted to stay at Grosvenor Square with a man who refused to even share a meal with her, then so be it. He would no longer spend his evenings there as he had the past two nights, but he could not return to Diane. Not after what he'd experienced with Isadore. Lastly, he was firmly resolved not to bed her again.

Even though the very idea of it aroused him.

* * *

Now that she didn't have to pretend to be an invalid anymore, Sophia descended the stairs to avail herself of William's library. What a cozy chamber it was with its dark woods, rich red Turkey carpets, rows of fine leather-bound books, and a fire blazing in the hearth.

She walked to William's desk and sat. She already missed him so dreadfully, she wished to feel his presence. What kind of penmanship did he possess? Would he keep a tidy desk? There on his mahogany desk was a leather ledger. Even though it wasn't her place to open it, she did. After all, if she hadn't already been married, she could be betrothed to William at this very minute, and one should be able to pry into one's husband's—or one's betrothed's—things. Shouldn't one? The memory of his proposal sent her heart soaring.

Instead of featuring columns of numbers, this ledger was a series of handwritten notes. William's hand? It had to be. There was no evidence of him having a secretary.

A shortened name at the top of the very first page caught her attention. *Ld Finkel.* Her stomach plunged. She read over all three pages of the notes, even though much of it was written in a peculiar shorthand that William must have devised.

It became clear that William vastly disliked Finkie and was attempting to enumerate the many people whose lives the vile Lord Finkel had destroyed.

Would William know of Lord Finkel's recent marriage? There had been no announcement in any of the newspapers. Since Sophia had never before met William, she didn't believe he moved in their social circles. Therefore, it was entirely possible that William was uninformed about Finkie's recent nuptials. Only three other people had attended the wedding—her two siblings who were in London and Lord Finkel's friend, the publisher Josiah Smith.

How did William know Finkie? Or had someone he cared for been ruined by Finkie? She could well imagine William championing a person crushed by the odious Lord Finkel. She believed William would lay down his life for a loved one. Even for her—before they'd ever been aware of this powerful love which bound them.

She must share the information with her brother. Perhaps he could use this to persuade Finkie to give her her freedom. She found paper and began to copy the pages.

When she finished, she went to Dottie's chamber, but she wasn't there. She was in Sophia's bedchamber, ironing.

This was the first time the lady and her maid

had come face to face since she'd dispatched Dottie to fetch her something to eat the previous night. Sophia effected a mock glare as she neared her supposed sister.

Dottie looked up from ironing her mistress's dress, a cocky expression on her slender face and a twinkle in her eye. "How do it feel to be a ruined woman?"

"If one is ruined by Mr. William Birmingham, the answer is . . . wonderful." She eyed Dottie and spoke somberly. "He asked me to marry him this morning."

"I do 'ope ye said yes. I've known since that first night he was the man for you."

"I couldn't possibly say yes. I'm already married."

The maid's face collapsed. "What did he have to say about that?"

"I couldn't tell him I was married. Then he would avoid me like the plague. And I couldn't have that."

"Lady Sophia Beresford's married, but Isadore ain't."

"What's that supposed to mean?" Sophia asked, dumbfounded.

"Couldn't Isadore marry him?"

"I am Isadore—sort of—and I most certainly cannot marry the man of my dreams because I'm already married."

"It's a lot to consider, what with all the mixed tales to keep up with—and not being able to talk, at that." Dottie set down her iron and began to carefully lay the freshly pressed dress in the clothes press. "I 'ave it!"

"What?" Sophia asked hopefully.

"I'll go around and tell Stinkie Finkie that you

have thoroughly ruined yourself with another man. Surely then he'll set you free."

Sophia shook her head. "I cannot allow that. Lord Finkel is noted for his temper. I fear he'd want to kill the messenger—that being you—and I would never permit that to happen."

Dottie sighed. "While ye was being ruined last night, I kept thinking how much I wish to be ruined by Mr. Thompson. But he would never make the first move 'cause he thinks I'm a fine lady above his touch. I can't even tell him I'm not. I can't tell him nothing."

"There are nonverbal ways to let him know you're interested."

"What's nonverbal mean?"

"Without talking."

"So you think I should just walk up and plant my lips on his?"

"Not at all! You must be subtle. Remember, he thinks you're a lady."

"What would you do that's subtle?"

"Let's say he accompanies you to my brother's house again—as I'm going to ask that he do—you link your arm to his. Allow his upper arm to rub against the side of your breasts. I'll own, yours aren't large, but there's enough there to differentiate you from the opposite gender." Sophia drew in a deep breath as she thought of William touching her own breasts. "Then you might consider patting his arm with your free hand. Not a pat like one would pet a dog but a slow, sensuous circular motion of your fingers. I truly believe such a small gesture would send him the message far more loudly than your voice could."

Dottie began fanning her face. "I get all hot and

excited just thinking about it."

Now Sophia fully understood those feelings.

"Go make yourself as lovely as possible whilst I pen another letter to my brother. Then I'll summon Thompson to escort you to Curzon Street to deliver it."

After Dottie returned to her chamber, Sophia sat at the desk and wrote.

Dearest Devere,

I am enclosing some damning information about Lord Finkel. I'm hoping you can find a way to use it to achieve our goal—the protection of Maryann's reputation AND the termination of my marriage agreement with the evil man.

Please come to me as soon as you learn anything. But not while Mr. Birmingham is here.

I feel as if my very life is in your hands. I beg that you bring me good tidings.

Your affectionate sister, S.

She wondered if she should have asked that her brother be the one to inform Finkie she was a thoroughly ruined woman, but she feared Devere would pluck her away from William and blame him as a debaucher of innocents.

She couldn't allow either of those occurrences.

After she gave her instructions to Thompson, who fortunately did not question why he needed Miss Dorothea Door's company to deliver a message, the two of them set off. Sophia sat at her chamber window looking out over the dreary day. She had to keep an eye out for the real Isadore, should she show up here. Sophia watched as Thompson assisted Dottie into a tilbury. How thoughtful he was to wish to keep Miss Dorothea Door from dragging her skirts through the wet, muddy streets. Now that it was raining rather vigorously, Sophia felt guilty for sending poor Dottie out in such weather.

She worried even more about her dear William, who'd gone off on horseback. He would get thoroughly soaked. She wondered who he'd be meeting, how long he'd be gone—all while watching for the real Isadore.

Would the woman physically resemble her? Sophia's tall casements kept getting fogged up and she was repeatedly obliged to clear them with a soft cloth.

Two hours slowly dragged by before Dottie returned. She came flying into her mistress's chamber, her face aglow. "I did it, milady!"

Sophia was not foolish enough to believe the delivery of her letter would account for Dottie's uncommon glee. She must have been subtly seductive with the valet. "I take it you achieved your aim?"

"You was right, milady! After I'd been stroking his arm in tender circles, subtle like, as you told me to do, he settled his hand most tenderly upon mine."

"Did he say anything?"

"Only with his actions. Remember, he still believes I'm a fine lady like yerself. He's far too proud."

"I think it's good that you're taking this slowly. Now, next time I ask him to accompany you, you'll initiate something a little more provocative than today's action."

"Like what?"

"Allow me to think on it for awhile. You know I'm not a quick thinker. Now, what of my brother? Did you see him?"

"He weren't in."

"Oh," Sophia said in a disappointed voice. "So you merely left my letter for him to read when he returns."

Dottie rolled her eyes. "I almost got found out when that Morris opened the door. He started to say something to me. Then he musta thought better of it, owing to my haughty look."

"That was fortunate. Were your Thompson to find out the truth, he'd tell William, and that could ruin everything for me."

Dottie came and settled a gentle hand on Sophia's shoulder. "I shouldn't like it if you was to end up like the unfortunate Lady Wapping."

"I have the good fortune to have you as my maid, my sister, and my dear friend."

Dottie looked across the chamber at the large tester bed. "I suppose ye'll be sharing yer bed with Mr. Birmingham tonight?"

"If he ever comes home." How could his blasted meeting take so wretchedly long?

Even after night came, she continued to sit at her window and peer out over Grosvenor Square. No sign of a woman who might be Isadore. No sign of William.

Something was wrong. This morning had been the happiest of her life. As evening set in, she was steeped in melancholy.

$\mathcal{C}$hapter 8

No less than three men in Lord Finkel's employ lingered discreetly along the block of stately homes that lined Curzon Street. One, a strapping lad of eighteen dressed in oilskins to repel the rain, appeared to be directing his full attention to his horse that had supposedly come up lame. Another, swathed in a greatcoat that was much too small for his considerable height, stood on the corner hawking hot chestnuts. The last of Finkel's employees eagerly watched conveyances speed past at the opposite corner, appearing to be waiting for someone. Which, indeed, he was.

All three were in possession of weapons which they would not hesitate to use in order to restore Lady Finkel to her husband. If that she-devil he'd wed even tried to seek refuge with her brother, Lord Finkel's men would immediately accost her.

Such knowledge should gratify said lord. But it did not.

Three nights had now passed since his ill-fated wedding night, and still he had not the slightest inkling of where that damned bride of his had fled. If his servants were to be believed, the witch had run off with a well-to-do giant of a man. What pleasure it would give Lord Finkel to have that wife stealer beaten to a pulp. Lord Finkel never had to resort to violence himself—not when he possessed legions of servants who did not object to undertaking his often illegal schemes.

Eyeing Devere's house from inside his coach, he drew a breath of impatience. How could plans he had painstakingly laid over the course of two years have gone so badly awry? Since he'd first set eyes on Lady Sophia at Almack's, he'd been driven by a desire to possess her by whatever means it would take.

This was the third day he'd come to Devere House to inquire about his wife's whereabouts. From her brother's shocked expression that first day, Finkel believed Lord Devere had no knowledge of his sister's flight.

The Finkel coachman opened his door and held an umbrella over the opening as his master disembarked. Lord Finkel took the umbrella in his own hands, strode to the glossy front door of Devere House, and rapped. A moment later, an elderly butler opened the door.

Though Finkel was accustomed to having his coachman announce him, today he wished to gauge the Devere servant's reaction. "Lord Finkel to see Lord Devere."

There was no change in the expression on the butler's face. "Lord Devere is not in."

Finkel shoved a shoe into the doorway. "Then I beg to wait within."

Now the butler's carefully controlled features crashed for a fraction of a second before he recovered. "Of course, my lord. I will show you to his lordship's library."

They strolled along the checkered marble entry hall where the walls were covered with portraits of long-dead Deveres stacked up the stairwell one on top of the other. When the two men reached the asparagus green library at the rear of the ground floor, the butler spoke in a feeble voice. "I cannot say when Lord Devere will return, my lord. It's possible that he may be gone all day."

Finkel passed a writing table and went to stand in front of the fire. "I understand."

As the butler went to leave the chamber, Finkel casually asked, "By the way, have you seen Lady Sophia?"

The servant's white head shook. "Not since the day she wed, my lord. She's greatly missed. Mrs. Blackpool—that would be our housekeeper—says it's as if the house is weeping for Lady Sophia. It's been so solemn and quiet since she left."

As soon as the door to the library closed, Finkel raced back to the writing table. When walking by it, he'd caught a glimpse of a letter written in Lady Sophia's hand. He snatched it from the top of the day's post. It was addressed to her brother.

He tore it open and began to read, but one phrase leapt off the page and struck terror in his heart: *damning information about Lord Finkel.* His pulse hammering and his curses lashing, he scanned the rest of the letter, then hurled it into the fire.

Drawing in a deep breath, he looked at the second sheet of paper—a list. It sickened him. Someone had managed to enumerate several of his blackmail schemes. There was Lady Audley's affair with her banker. There was the matter of card cheating instigated by Lord Smithington at White's, and a land swindle by Sir Percy Yarborough.

Who could possibly have known that he used his knowledge of these potentially damning scandals to increase his own wealth? He turned the next page over. Several more potential scandals he'd averted—for a price—were listed.

He would be ruined if this information was ever released. It was imperative that he find the author of this list.

He wished he hadn't thrown the bitch's note into the fire. Hadn't she mentioned a Mr. Birmingham? She'd written for her brother to come to her, but not if Mr. Birmingham were home. That must mean she was staying with Birmingham. He had to be the wealthy giant she'd run off with.

There was a sudden lurch in his gut. There lived in the capital an extremely wealthy man named Birmingham, Nicholas Birmingham. And he was considerably taller than average. The stockbroker was said to be the wealthiest man in England.

Lord Finkel's resources could never compete with those of the Birminghams.

Had Nicholas Birmingham not married Lady Fiona Hollingsworth the previous year? Why would he be aiding Lady Sophia?

Lord Finkel had to find out if the stockbroker was the man with whom Lady Finkel had run off. Most important of all, he must uncover the identity of the man who'd been stalking him.

That man must die.

* * *

Sophia spent the better part of the day wiping the windows in her bedchamber so she could see if the real Isadore came to Grosvenor Square. She was obliged to put on her thick velvet cloak because the frigid air seemed to be pouring into her chamber from the slender casement. The freezing glass also necessitated that she don kid gloves.

She could not recall ever being so bored. She could paint from memory each house on the north side of Grosvenor Square. She had learned the corresponding number to each one of the homes. She'd memorized the distinctive friezes of every mansion on Grosvenor Square. She knew the first house on the north corner was stuccoed in cream, the second of Portland stone

If even one nurse with her charge had entered the park in the center of the square, it would have relieved Sophia's boredom, but on so rainy a day, she had not even that small diversion.

Not for a single moment the entire day did the relentless rain let up. Fortunately, Dottie and her protector suffered no ill effects from their visit to Curzon Street. Upon her servant's return, Sophia had ordered her to change into dry clothes.

The only bright spot in Sophia's dreary day occurred after Dottie had donned a fresh dress and flew into her mistress's chamber, bursting with excitement.

A smile tweaking at her lips, her eyes narrowed in mock consternation, Sophia addressed her maid. "I perceive that Thompson was receptive to your affections."

In her gleeful state, the slender Dottie could almost appear pretty. Though every one of her forty years was etched into her angular face, the sprinkle of freckles upon her nose and the coppery tresses unspoiled by gray lent a more youthful aspect to her countenance. Her green eyes shimmered with childish delight. "Oh, yes, milady!"

"Did you trace slow, sensuous circles upon his arm?"

Unable to suppress her grin, Dottie's head

bobbed in the affirmative.

"Did he do anything or say anything?"

"Not at first. At first he was all silent, but after a while—when he could see that I was intentionally sending a *nonverbal* signal—something in him seemed to change. He didn't say nothin' but it was as if his step was lighter, and a smile fixed upon his face."

"I can't recall ever seeing the man smile."

"Me neither. That was his *nonverbal* way of telling me how pleased he was by my actions."

"He never said anything to you about your . . . your actions?"

Dottie shook her head.

"Did he by chance attempt to give you any nonverbal signals?"

"Indeed he did." Had Dottie just received a proposal from a prince she could not have appeared any happier.

Sophia cocked her head. "Are you going to tell me about it?"

Dottie sighed. "It made me so happy, I love recalling it. I thought me heart would burst."

"Out with it."

"He put his hand over mine and clasped it like for quite a long period of time. He's so big his hand's twice the size of mine. Then when we reached the door at Devere House, he put his arm around me, just as if we was 'usband and wife. I ain't never felt so good before. I felt like he was my very own protector. I felt . . . I felt like I 'aven't felt since I was rocked in me mama's arms a great long time ago."

Sophia's heart softened. "You felt cherished."

Dottie nodded. "That's the very word I was looking for! You know, there's a lot to be said for *nonverbal* communication."

Sophia thought of all the silent ways she had shown William how much he meant to her. "Indeed there is."

"So, milady, do you have any more advice on what I'm to do next to send Mr. Thompson an affectionate *nonverbal* message?"

Sophia considered the request for a moment. She'd never been a quick thinker. She pondered how she would convey her affection to William in a nonverbal way, and an idea suddenly leapt to her mind. "When you're riding in a carriage together, you could set a hand upon his thigh."

Dottie's eyes rounded. "And make those slow, sultry circles on his leg, you mean?"

Sophia nodded. "It would be very provocative."

"Just thinkin' about it steals me breath away!"

That conversation with Dottie had taken place hours ago.

Still, William had not returned. Where had he gone? Had he taken a warm coat? Had he managed to protect himself from the chilled rain? The rumble of distant thunder made her even more morose. Had something happened to her beloved? Had he no regard for his good health? Riding in this abominable weather could send him to bed with fever—or even worse.

Sophia's thoughts continued to flit to his proposal that first morning at Grosvenor Square. How could something that made her so happy then now meld into something so melancholy? Had she merely dreamed that William wanted to marry her? She'd held a deep conviction in his sincerity. Now, her trust in him wavered. Had he truly felt they belonged together, he would not have stayed away all day. Would he not wish to be with her as acutely as she longed to be with him?

The day grew darker and darker. Neither her brother nor her lover came. Her melancholy magnified. She was certain something was wrong. She feared that something threatened William. Whatever had happened, she instinctively knew, would destroy the bliss she'd known that morning, would sever that bond that forged them together as if they'd shared a single heartbeat.

Dottie came and tried to persuade her to eat, but Sophia refused. The anxiety that seeped through her like the most potent brandy had unsettled her stomach.

Night fell early this time of the year. By four o'clock the already dark skies had become completely black, save for the lanterns flanking the doorways across the square. Just as her aunt's footman was lighting the lamps at Number 12, a lone horseman rode into the square. She would know him amidst a thousand riders. Even covered by a voluminous woolen greatcoat and a hat smashed on his golden locks, he could not conceal those exceptionally broad shoulders or those powerful thighs straddling the beast. He sat a horse as he did everything—emanating a sense of command. He was the kind of man one would turn to in a crisis. As, indeed, she had.

As his mount trotted up to his narrow house, she recalled how masterfully he had dispatched Finkie's violent henchmen, and her heart swelled. She pictured him handily overpowering two men as one would squash an insect.

William was her fate. She believed he must have been put on this earth to share her life, to be her protector, her lover. He was meant to save her from the vile Lord Finkel. No other man but

William would ever do.

As a footman raced from the house to take William's horse, she leapt from her settee and hurried from her room, her heartbeat scurrying at the prospect of beholding this man who had come to mean so much to her. She flew down the stairs, and when she neared the entry hall, she halted and watched as he handed off his sodden coat to the butler. His breeches were soaked as if they'd been immersed in a lake.

As she drew closer, she saw that the normally tanned skin of his face had turned a ruddy red from exposure, and he shivered. She watched as he peeled off wet leather gloves. His icy fingers were numb.

The contrast between the way he looked when he'd left that morning and the way he looked now caused her heartbeat to skid. He looked as if he'd been caught in a cyclone. It wasn't just the obvious exposure to raw elements that accounted for his bedraggled appearance. It was as if the confidence that had defined him had been torn away.

She moved to him, her brows lowered. "I've been worried about you all day, and now it seems my fears were warranted. Why did you expose yourself to such beastly weather? You'll take a lung infection." She wanted to be held in his arms, but she knew he would never allow such a display in front of his servants. Instead, she went to slip her arm into his, but he stiffed and elbowed her away.

His coolness stung. "I beg that you come up and sit before the fire in my chamber," she said in a gentle voice. "You must be chilled to the marrow."

"I thank you, but I have duties which require my attention." He began to climb the stairs. "Fenton, I shall need a hot bath immediately."

"As you wish, Mr. Birmingham."

Her pulse skittered at the thought of those powerful golden limbs of his sliding into the bath. She pictured the way his bare body had looked in firelight, her breath catching in her chest. How she longed to be the one to trickle warm water over the body that had given her such pleasure the previous night. She could not allow herself to dwell on lathering soap over his barreled chest or to imagine her fingers combing through his hair—not when an obvious change of heart had come over him.

As she silently followed him up the stairs, she felt like a mongrel who'd just been kicked by its master. *What have I done?* Why his sudden iciness?

As upset as she was over his stiffness to her, she was just as worried about his well-being. Had he been riding in the rain all this chilly winter day? Her mind raced to her acquaintances who had succumbed to consumption before their twenty-fifth birthdays.

When he reached the second floor and started for his bedchamber, she spoke. "You must drink some hot tea, dress warmly, and cover yourself with blankets."

He stopped and slowly turned toward her, a frosty expression on his handsome face. "Save your regard for your husband."

$\mathcal{C}$hapter 9

Even though it was but four o'clock, it was almost completely dark by the time Lord Finkel reached Nicholas Birmingham's establishment on Threadneedle Street. It was a wicked day to be out in the elements. Curse that wench he'd married! When the coachman went to open the door, the wind whipped it from his hand. Cursing under his breath, Finkel snatched the umbrella away from his well-meaning servant. Even with an umbrella, he was in for a thorough drenching. And it was beastly cold.

The old red brick building in which Nicholas Birmingham conducted his business—when he wasn't at the Exchange—did not look like the establishment of one who was said to be the richest man in the kingdom. The interior with its plain utilitarianism was even more shocking. No Turkey carpets on the cold stone floor, and one solitary writing table behind which sat a youthful, bespectacled clerk.

"May I help you?" the fellow asked.

"Lord Finkel to see Mr. Birmingham."

"You are expected?"

"No, but it's imperative that I speak to him."

"Perhaps there's something I can assist you with. All orders for Mr. Birmingham come though me."

Lord Finkel glared. "The matter I wish to

discuss with Mr. Birmingham is of a personal nature."

The young man rose. "Very well. I'll go see if he has a few minutes to spare."

Finkel had never before met the rich stockbroker, never spoken with him, but he had seen him and his beautiful wife—the former Lady Fiona Hollingsworth, an earl's daughter—at Almack's.

A moment later, the clerk came from his employer's office. "You may go in, my lord."

Birmingham stood when Finkel entered. Even though Finkel had been prepared to be condescending to the Cit, he was unaccountably taken aback. In this man's presence, Finkel felt small, even inadequate. Nicholas Birmingham was said to be the most handsome man in London. Finkel could well believe it. The man was probably six foot three, with broad shoulders and lanky frame. There was nothing objectionable in his face. In fact, the man had been blessed to be born with excellent, very white teeth and an aquiline nose. His colouring was dark, with deep brown hair, black eyes and dark complexion like those from Mediterranean countries.

"How can I be of assistance to you, my lord?" Birmingham asked. Though his words were polite, the tone of his voice was stiff to the point of being disparaging.

"I won't beat around the bush. I've come to fetch my wife."

A puzzled look crossed the taller man's face. "I beg your pardon? I know nothing of your wife."

Finkel had suspected that Nicholas Birmingham would be a fool to be unfaithful to his beautiful Lady Fiona. The woman was perfection.

Then suddenly he remembered there was another Birmingham brother. "Then it must be your brother who runs the Birmingham family bank."

"If you think my brother Adam has run off with your wife, I assure you that you're delusional. I see my brother every day, and I am certain you are mistaken."

"If I learn that you've lied to me, Birmingham, I'll do everything in my power to bring down the House of Birmingham."

Birmingham's eyes narrowed, and he spoke in a steely manner. "Leave at once."

Finkel returned Birmingham's icy glare, then turned and stormed to the door.

He had only to go a few doors down to reach the Birmingham's bank, where he demanded to speak to Adam Birmingham on a personal matter.

This brother's office bespoke the family's vast wealth. There were Turkey carpets, a Canaletto on the wall, rich mahogany furnishings and plush velvet-covered chairs. Crystal chandeliers hung from the ceiling.

When Finkel came face to face with Adam Birmingham, he felt almost as if he were seeing the twin of Nicholas Birmingham. The slight differences between the two were difficult to articulate. Perhaps it was something about the mouth that distinguished one from the other, or perhaps it was the cut of their chins. Both were tall and dark and would be considered to be in possession of a handsome countenance. This brother seemed more personable than the other.

He bowed, smiled at Finkel, and quirked a brow. "You wished to see me on a personal matter?"

Finkel stepped into his luxurious office and

silently closed the door behind them. "Indeed. My wife has run off with a Mr. Birmingham, and I want her back."

Adam Birmingham began to laugh. "I assure you, my lord, I've not run off with your wife or with any man's wife."

"You do fit the description of the man with whom my wife eloped."

"I don't normally discuss my personal affairs with anyone, but allow me to say I am happy with my present domestic situation."

"Then you are married?"

"I didn't say that."

It was then that Finkel remembered. About a year earlier he'd heard that the beautiful Italian opera singer Anna Cannales had come under Adam Birmingham's protection.

Finkel had been certain this was the man who had stolen his wife, but he believed he—and his brother—had spoken the truth. The Birminghams had a reputation for getting what they wanted, and if one of them wanted Lady Sophia Beresford, he would have had no qualms about admitting it.

He'd wasted the whole bloody afternoon—and unnecessarily exposed himself to the brutal elements.

"Then I'm sorry to have taken your time."

Once more, Finkel angrily stormed from a Birmingham establishment.

Where the devil was the Birmingham with whom his wife had run off? Finkel would not stop until he found him.

* * *

It would serve her right if he did take lung fever and die! The blame for his foolish drenching in sub-freezing temperatures rested solely on her delicate shoulders.

William found himself wishing he hadn't gone to MacIver that morning, hadn't learned that she belonged to another. If only he could recapture that heady sense of possession he'd felt that morning at the thought of plighting his life to hers.

Though he'd thought he did not want to be married, once the idea of wedding Isadore had taken root, he had been steeped in a rush of almost unbearable joy. It was as if he'd waited the whole of his life to find the perfect mate.

And he'd found her in Isadore.

With the exception of her criminal livelihood, she was perfection. Beauty, intelligence, and sublime sexual compatibility all combined in one exquisite being.

One exquisite being who belonged to an honorable man. Lord Evers.

How could she have so thoroughly fooled William? He had been convinced she spoke the truth when she'd told him she was a maiden. Then, when they made love the first of many times, he would have sworn she had never lain with another man.

And in no way did she act like a woman married to another. Last night, this morning, and even a few moments ago, her words and actions were those of a woman who sincerely loved him.

He should not have come home. He should have stayed at his club and sent for Thompson to bring around dry clothing. Seeing her had been far too painful—especially when her very countenance bespoke tender affection toward him. The woman could rival Sarah Siddons on the stage.

He pictured her as she looked when she met him in the entry hall. How difficult it had been not to draw her within his arms when he'd stood there in the entry corridor and gazed up at her stunning beauty, at the tender concern in her face and in her voice. In spite of his physical discomfort, the sight of her aroused him. He groaned.

He would never again know the feel of her silken flesh. He respected Lord Evers far too much to take liberties with his wife.

Even if that wife did act as if she were in love with William. MacIver must have been right about her serial affairs. How convincing she'd been!

Thompson helped remove William's soggy boots, then tested the bath water whilst William peeled off the rest of his wet clothing. "Did Miss Isadore Door have any more callers today?" he asked casually.

"No, my lord, but she once again dispatched me—along with Miss Dorothea Door—to that house on Curzon Street."

William wondered if that was where Lord Evers resided. Owing to the fact Evers spent most of his time out of the country, William's only interaction with the peer had been during several visits to the Hague. Now that he thought about it, he realized Evers fit the description Thompson had given him of Isadore's caller of the previous day: a tall, well dressed man of the higher classes. "With another note?" William lowered his shivering body into the metal tub. As he became immersed in the warm water, his chills vanished. God, but he'd thought of this all day long. This and lying with Isadore.

"Yes." Thompson folded his toweling and set it on a stool next to the tub. "My lord, I wonder if I could speak to you of something that's private in nature."

"I doubt I have any secrets from you."

"This actually pertains to me. To me and Miss Door."

William's spine stiffened. "Isadore?"

"Oh, no my lord. Miss Dorothea Door."

William pictured the aging, bony, utterly plain sister and felt sorry for her. "What about her?"

Thompson cleared his throat. "It would appear that the lady's taken a fancy to me."

The poor woman. Thompson was likely the only man who'd ever directed any attentions at her. "I expect it's because you've shown her such kindness."

"She does bring out traits in me I did not know I possessed. She makes me feel as if I could slay dragons to protect her."

William's eyes widened. Could it be possible that Thompson was attracted to the unfortunate spinster? It was almost incomprehensible to William that any man could find something to admire in the homely sister. He supposed it showed there was, indeed, someone for everyone. "Dear lord, Thompson, do you fancy her?"

"Indeed I do, my lord, but she's too highborn for the likes of me."

"It's not as if she's an aristocrat. Her scheming sister regularly conducts criminal activities."

"There is that."

William no longer pitied the plain sister. Perhaps she and Thompson could be happy together. "If she fancies you, you must take that as permission to court her."

"But I haven't the slightest idea how one goes about courting a woman."

"No one tells the birds and bees what to do.

Permit yourself to follow your instincts." William's thoughts trailed to the previous night when his and Isadore's potent instincts had led them to a place of unimaginable happiness.

"I think I should very much like to kiss the lady. Do you think it would be improper?"

William's face screwed in thought. "Tell me, if she cannot speak how did the lady convey her feelings to you?"

The firelight from the nearby fireplace illuminated Thompson's face. Was the fellow blushing?

He stammered for a moment. "The lady placed her hand upon my forearm, and began to rub me in a tender, circular motion. At first I thought it was unintentional, but as it continued for a considerable period of time, I began to believe that the lady was . . . well, exceedingly comfortable with me."

William began to guffaw. "She's a saucy little dish who's undoubtedly smitten with you, old boy."

"I shall defer to your judgment since you have considerably more experience in such matters than I."

There could be no happy ending for William and Isadore, but it oddly satisfied him to think the unfortunate mute might find love so late in life. "You and Miss Dorothea Door have my blessing."

* * *

Even though she had no appetite, Sophia sent Dottie off with a note to Fenton inquiring if the master were dining at home that night. Her heart plummeted when Dottie came back and informed her that Mr. Birmingham had asked for a tray in his room.

He's avoiding me.

She could not blame him. Were she in his place she knew how betrayed she would have felt upon learning—after their night of tender passion—that he was married. If only she could convey to him how dearly she loved him. If only she could tell him her marriage had never been and never would be consummated.

But what did that matter? Whether she wanted it or not, she was irrevocably united with a detestable man. That must explain why Devere had not come to her that day. His solicitor must have told him that it was not possible to extricate Sophia from her marriage to Lord Finkel. Knowing her determined brother, she thought it possible he would not concede to Finkie without putting up a valiant fight.

She sent Dottie away and flung herself, prostrate, upon her bed, tears trickling down her cheeks as she contemplated William's coolness to her. It suddenly occurred to her that though William had found out she was married, in all likelihood, he'd actually found out *Isadore* was married.

Would that change anything? She wept. It changed nothing. For nothing could nullify the reality that she was, in the laws of Britain, Lady Finkel.

She sighed. A week ago she'd been ignorant of love. A week ago she'd had no experience with the pain of lost love. A week ago her life was so dull she had settled for a man she could neither admire nor love.

Bitter cries rung from her. Had she to do it all over again would she have opened herself up to this unimaginable pain caused by the loss of

William's affections? Yes, she still would have chosen a night of sin with William. For one night she had known the love of a man who was far and away above all others.

Would it help if she could make William understand he was the only man she'd ever loved? She doubted it. Men enjoyed possession, and as long as she was Lady Finkel, a proud man like William would never be satisfied.

She was not willing to leave his house. Once she was gone, she knew their paths were unlikely to ever again cross. And she could not bear that.

Her only hope of clinging to some part of him was to continue posing as Isadore. Even if Isadore was married. As long as he needed the gold Isadore could produce, he would allow her to remain under his roof. She vowed that either she or Dottie would keep a vigil at the window looking for the real Isadore.

But what made her think Isadore would work with her? She would have to persuade Devere to come up with funds for Isadore—on the promise that all would be repaid once William paid the imposter Isadore eighty thousand pounds.

She leapt from her bed and scribbled a note begging her brother to get his hands on eighty thousand quid which could possibly be repaid within a week. Dottie wasn't in her chamber. Never one to miss a meal—despite her skinniness—she must be dining alone in the dinner room.

Sophia found her there and explained that she and Thompson must make yet another trip to Curzon Street that very night.

Dottie's face brightened, and she whispered. "I'll get to try that *nonverbal* leg rubbin'!"

Sophia's gaze fanned over the mountain of food upon her maid's plate. "Not if you continue sitting here all night stuffing yourself."

Dottie pushed the plate aside and rose from the table. "I'll take me Mr. Thompson over food any night."

"I'll send a footman to seek Thompson—if his master will permit him to undertake a commission for us."

"I 'ope he do let him."

Apparently William had no objections to lending the ladies Thompson's services. Minutes later, Dottie and the valet were off to Curzon Street. It was hopeless for Sophia to try to talk to William tonight. He'd made it very clear he wanted nothing to do with her.

He had to know that what had occurred last night was not the whim of a promiscuous married woman. She owed him some kind of explanation. She returned to the desk in her chamber and began to pen a letter written from depths of heart.

* * *

When Dottie reached the bottom of the stairs, dear Mr. Thompson was standing there in the entry hall looking ever so handsome as he smiled up at her. There was such affection upon his face, she felt like a lovely fairy princess.

"I've sent around for the carriage. I shouldn't like a delicate thing like you exposed to the elements, my dear Miss Door."

A delicate thing like you. She hoped he never saw her slaving over a hot iron. She did so fancy the idea of him thinking her a lady. A *delicate* lady. Perhaps these days at Grosvenor Square would merely be a fling to brighten the rest of her days with warm memories. She hated to think of revealing her true identity to this gentleman.

He helped her put on a thick woolen cape and tenderly covered her head with its hood. "It's beastly cold outside."

When the coach came they left the house. She shivered instantly. She'd known it was cold but hadn't been prepared for the icy wind that seemed to cut right through her like a sharpened icicle.

As she stepped into the coach, she was seized with nervousness. Once again like that night she'd had to leap from Stinkie Finkie's roof. Would she have the nerve to set her hand to Mr. Thompson's powerful thigh? Now that it was time to implement such an action, it occurred to her that by doing so, she would appear to be a doxy. She didn't want Mr. Thompson to think her a loose woman.

Then she recalled the finest lady she knew— Lady Sophia—acting far more bold with Mr. Birmingham—and he had asked her to marry him! Of course Dottie weren't a beauty like Lady Sophia.

But what woman wouldn't want a proposal from the man she was in love with?

She took a seat on the leather bench, and Mr. Thompson sat across from her. How right he'd been about the beastly cold. Even within the coach, it was freezing. How much warmer she would be were he sitting here beside her.

"I'm sorry this is just a rented, serviceable coach—not luxurious like Mr. Birmingham's that was destroyed the other day. I suppose you're accustomed to finer than this."

How she wished she could talk! She wanted him to know she didn't expect luxury or riches. Her stomach dropping like a rock, her heartbeat hammering, she rose and plopped herself down next to him.

Before she could summon the neve to set her trembling hand to his thigh, he turned to her. "My dearest Miss Door, would you permit me to kiss you?"

She felt as if one of those huge church bells had gone off in her chest. Could he hear it? Her smile widened. Would he think her too bold? She attempted to nod in a most decorous fashion.

Mr. Thompson drew in a breath and settled one arm around her as he moved closer and lowered his lips to hers. His lips were so much softer than she would have expected on a big man like him. And ever so tender, especially for a big man like him.

She was self-conscious that she wouldn't know how to kiss. Would he be able to tell? Nevertheless, she puckered her lips to his and basked in the warm glow of the pleasure he was giving her. She forgot how bitterly cold it was outside for snuggled against Mr. Thompson she could never be cold.

Then the coach pulled up in front of Devere House, and he terminated the kiss. "You needn't go out in this cold, Miss Door. I'll deliver the note." He tucked a rug about her lap and left.

On weddings of members of the Devere family she had been permitted to drink champagne. It made her feel all bubbly inside. That's exactly how she felt as she sat there in the coach.

He was only gone for a moment. When he returned to sit beside her, he sighed. "A pity the ride from Grosvenor Square to Curzon Street is so short." Then he turned to her and once again drew her into his arms.

This second kiss was even more passionate.

$\mathcal{C}$hapter 10

"Did you see my brother?" an anxious Sophia asked Dottie when she returned.

"No, milady. He weren't in, but Mr. Thompson left orders that your note was to be delivered to the master as soon as he returned."

Sophia's probing eyes studied her servant. The gleam in her maid's eye told her that Dottie had something to communicate about her own romantic pursuits. "You went in the coach because of the rain and cold?"

A smile on her face, Dottie nodded.

"Did you sit opposite from Thompson?"

"At first I did. Then I got up me courage and plopped meself down right next to him."

"And did the man show a reaction?"

"Indeed he did! He turned to me, a smile on his face, and he asked if he could kiss me. I didn't even have to rub his legs none to loosen him up."

"You permitted him to kiss you?"

Dottie directed an outraged glare at her mistress while setting hands to waist, elbows at right angles. "My mama didn't raise no slow tops. Of course I allowed him to kiss me!"

Sophia directed a brilliant smile at her. It was good to have something over which one could glow. "Did you enjoy it?"

"I enjoyed the kissing very much, and I believe me dear Mr. Thompson did too."

"Did he perchance initiate any *verbal* communications about your . . . intimacy?"

"If yer asking if he discussed our intimacy, then the answer's yes. He said my affections toward him were very agreeable to him. The pity of it was the drive to Curzon Street is exceedingly short."

Sophia giggled. "So you're saying you would like to have continued kissing your Mr. Thompson?" She thought of how she longed to kiss William.

"I most certainly would have!"

"Did he attempt to set up another sort of *meeting* with you?"

"I'll 'ave you know me Mr. Thompson's a gentleman who would not try to take liberties with a maiden. He did *not* ask if he could come to me bedchamber."

"Of course he wouldn't. He thinks you're a fine lady. Look at your dress."

Dottie frowned. "Your dress, you mean. What worries me is that when he eventually learns that I'm no fine gentlewoman, I'll lose his affections."

"I will own that's a possibility, but there are many facets to physical attraction, and I don't believe you could have engaged the man's affections if there had not been several things about you that appealed to him."

"I 'ope you're right. I know it's hard for me to understand just what there is about Mr. Thompson that has attracted me since the moment we met at the Prickly Pig. No upper servant at Devere House ever appealed to me as does Mr. Thompson. At first, it was that I found him 'andsome. I've always fancied men who are tall. But it's so much more than his physical appearance. He's got such an air about him. He's refined. He's courageous. He's . . . I think you'd use the word *solicitous* of my happiness."

Though Sophia could not agree that the valet was handsome, Thompson did possess the other traits that Dottie admired. She recalled how valiantly master and servant had fought side by side against Finkie's armed henchmen that day. "Your Mr. Thompson is brave and strong and just the sort of man a woman can lean on."

"When we parted, he said he 'oped you had another commission we could do together." Dottie lowered her voice. "He said he 'oped it would continue raining so that we could ride together inside a carriage. I ain't never before longed for rain, but I do now."

Sophia broke out laughing. Over the many years of their acquaintance the two women had frequently lamented rainy days.

Her mirth dissolved when her thoughts turned to William's drenching in this miserable weather. She prayed he would not be adversely affected by the intense cold and wet. It had been raining and cold on the day of their return to London, and none of them—fortunately—had suffered ill health.

This long, rainy day that had started out so wonderfully had turned into one of the dreariest days of her life.

After Dottie went to her own bedchamber, Sophia thought about the letter she'd written to William. She dared not deliver it—or have it delivered—tonight. Perhaps he would not be as angry the next day. Perhaps she could have Dottie relay the letter to Thompson, who could then see that William received it.

* * *

She awakened the following morning to the

splattering of rain upon her window. Her fire had gone out, and the room was so cold that the prospect of removing herself from beneath her blankets was most unwelcome.

Her thoughts went to Dottie, who had never for the past quarter of a century been permitted to lie in bed once the sun was up. How fortunate Sophia was to have been born into such privileged circumstances. All her life she'd been blessed in so many ways.

Until the fateful day she'd made the disastrous decision to wed Finkie.

This morning dear Dottie was a great deal more fortunate than her mistress. She was at liberty to fall in love with the man who owned her heart. The man returned her affections.

Fully dressed in Sophia's pale yellow morning gown, Dottie practically bounced into Sophia's adjacent room. Sophia forced herself to sit up. "Pray, hand me my shawl. I'm freezing."

Dottie went to the linen press and retrieved it. "No wonder yer so cold. The fire's gone out. I'll see to it."

"This morning I should like for you to deliver to Thompson a note for Mr. Birmingham."

Though her back was to Sophia as she built a new fire, Sophia could see a corner of her mouth lifted into a smile. "It's always a pleasure for me to see me Mr. Thompson."

Once the fire was lit, she turned to her mistress. "Now, let me 'elp you get dressed. What should ye like to wear today?

"The blue. I suppose I should have Devere bring me more clothes. With two of us wearing the dresses in my trousseau, there is little left in the way of selection." She observed Dottie with an eye to how she wore a gentlewoman's dress. "By the way, Dot, that dress is very becoming on you. I've decided that whenever we leave this house and you are at liberty to speak again, you shall have all my last season's dresses to wear every day." Sophia climbed from her bed, shivering, and moved to the fire.

"Oh, milady! That would be wonderful. Then Mr. Thompson wouldn't have to see me in drab servants' wear."

Sophia nodded. "I suppose by then he will know all there is to know about your proper identity, but until that day comes I shall beg you to stay my mute sister. I know it's difficult, but it cannot last much longer." She peered at the window. "One of us must watch the window all day every day until the real Isadore shows up."

"I'm sure I'll know her. She must look just like you."

"We know no such thing!"

Dottie's shoulders sagged. "That must be why Mr. Birmingham mistook you for her."

Sophia shook her head. "I believe he had no notion of what she looked like."

For the next ten minutes Sophia allowed her maid to assist in dressing for the day, though it mattered not what she wore. She would have to cover herself in her torn cape if she was to spend the day beside the frigid window.

When they were finished, Dottie moved to the looking glass and peered at herself.

"Your Mr. Thompson will be most pleased with your appearance. Now run along and deliver my letter." Sophia pointed to her writing desk. "It's right there."

Ten minutes passed before Dottie returned.

"Mr. Thompson assured me he would see that his master gets your letter, but he's away from home at present."

A deep melancholy washed over her. Though she had known William wished to avoid her, she had allowed herself to hope he would rush to her after reading the letter that revealed her tender affections.

Seconds later, she recovered enough to think clearly. "Then if William's out, it's imperative that my brother come to me this morning. You and Thompson must fetch him."

"But Mr. Birmingham will have taken the coach. I fear I'd take me death of cold out in this rain and cold."

Sophia scribbled a note, then went to her reticule and extracted some coins, handing them to Dottie. "Thompson must procure a hackney. I've put that in this note for him."

* * *

An hour later, Devere was greeting the sister who was closest to him in age. "Do you have any idea what hour it is?"

Sophia giggled. "I will own, my dear brother, that I've never seen you up so early since you left Oxford."

His dark eyes narrowed. "Even at Oxford I never rose this early."

He came to sit next to her on the settee which had been scooted up to a window—the window from which Sophia kept peering.

Even though he was her brother, it was impossible for her not to see why he was so highly sought after by every unmarried lady in the *ton*. Not only was he titled, but he was uncommonly handsome.

He had the look of one who was accustomed to commanding. Even his height was above average, and he filled out his well-tailored clothing in an utterly manly way. He shared Sophia's colouring of deep brown hair and eyes that were almost black. There was something about his face that revealed his excellent sense of humor and his propensity to smile.

But he was not smiling today.

"What the deuce are you looking at?" he asked.

Sophia turned away from peering out onto Grosvenor Square and sighed as she began to tell him about Isadore and the mistaken identities. "It's imperative that I remain Isadore until the exchange."

"So that's why you needed the bloody eighty thousand quid!"

She nodded.

"I can't lay my hands on that much money."

"Oh, but you must find a way. I swear to you, I'll pay it back as soon as Mr. Birmingham pays me the eighty thousand. It would not be more than a week away."

"What do you really know about this Birmingham? For all we know, he could slay you once he gets his hands on the gold."

She shook her head adamantly. "William would never do that. He's an honorable man."

Devere glared at her through narrowed eyes. "Christian names?"

"It's how I think of him. I assure you, he properly refers to me as Miss Door."

Her brother chuckled over the name *Door*. "How could you possibly know he's an honorable man? He's a smuggler, for pity's sake! He could end up in Newgate!"

Sophia got up. "Pray, sit here for a moment and watch for Isadore." She went and fetched Dottie and paraded her in front of Devere. "Dottie, I beg that you be honest. Tell my brother if you think Mr. Birmingham would take possession of the gold, then murder me."

Dottie's already large eyes rounded even more, then she faced the man responsible for her salary. "I swear to you, my lord, Mr. Birmingham do be a very fine man."

Sophia glared at her brother. "Dottie is possessed of unerring instincts about men. She begged me not to marry Lord Finkel."

Devere smiled at Dottie. "How I wish my sister had listened to you."

Dottie curtsied, then returned to her own chambers.

Her brother eyed Sophia suspiciously. "Why is it imperative that you stay here?"

She could hardly tell him that she had fallen passionately in love with the home's owner. Then her brother would know she'd behaved as a strumpet. It suddenly occurred to her that if Devere knew she'd been ruined, he could convey that information to Lord Finkel, and it might help convince that horrid man to let her go.

On the other hand, if Devere knew William Birmingham had compromised his maidenly sister, he might insist on removing her from the suspected seducer's house. Not only that, he would then be predisposed to think poorly of William. And she couldn't have that. William was noble of character.

Even if he did engage in activities outside the law.

"I am very comfortable here," she said. "As you

can see, it's a fine home. And since Mr. Birmingham does not move in our circles, Finkie will never think to look for me here. I will never go back to Lord Finkel. Speaking of Finkie, what did your solicitor have to say about my . . . " She hated to say the word. She swallowed. "My marriage."

Her heartbeat drumming, she eyed her brother.

A grimace flashed across his square face. "It doesn't look good, Soph. That's why I didn't come to you yesterday. To his knowledge, the marriage cannot be broken."

"Even for non-consummation?"

He shook his head. "Rutherford said he would study case law in the hopes of finding something you can use to break the marriage, but he's not hopeful."

"Then it's a very good thing we've been able to find out about Lord Finkel's illegal, unethical, villainous activities. We should be able to hold those over his head in exchange for my freedom."

Devere's brows lowered. "Pray, what in the devil are you talking about?"

"About the list I sent you yesterday."

"I never received any list from you."

"Of course you did. Dottie delivered it during the afternoon, but you were out."

"What kind of list?"

"I found on Mr. Birmingham's desk a ledger which enumerated various blackmail schemes carried out by Lord Finkel. I copied it and sent it to you. I knew you'd know what to do with that information."

"You mean Maryann wasn't the only one?"

"Exactly."

Devere cursed under his breath. "A pity they

don't draw and quarter such unscrupulous men any more. It looks as if I should join forces with your Mr. Birmingham to expose Finkel's foul deeds."

"When the time comes, yes. But for now Lord Finkel can't know you're the Earl of Devere."

He shook his head. "I almost gave away myself to your Mr. Birmingham's butler, but I caught myself just in time to announce myself as Mr. Beresford."

She'd hardly paid attention to her brother. She'd couldn't get her mind off why he had not received yesterday's letter. Her eyes narrowed. "My letter must be on your desk. Isn't that where Cummings always puts your post?"

"He does, but it's not there. I read all my post when I returned late yesterday." He began to curse, making no effort to shield her from hearing his words.

It had been years since she'd seen her brother so angry. "What's the matter?"

"It's that damned Finkel!"

It was if an explosion jolted her chest. "He was at our . . . I mean *your* house yesterday?" If that were the case, that meant Finkie knew about William's list. Her heart roared so loud she would not be surprised if her brother could hear it. *Dear God, that could put William's life in jeopardy!* She distinctly remembered that her cover letter said to come to Mr. Birmingham's house.

Now, Finkel had a name.

Devere nodded. "I wasn't in, but Cummings said the blackguard insisted on waiting for my return. Shortly after Cummings showed him to my library, he hurriedly left the house. That no-good spawn of the devil stole my letter!"

"He must have recognized my handwriting," she said in a somber voice, shaking her head. "Would that I'd never met the evil man."

"Could you try to copy that damning list again?" he asked.

"If it's still on Mr. Birmingham's writing table I will."

Devere sighed. "I'll go to my banker and see if I can lay my hands on eighty thousand quid."

"I hope it will be needed."

"What if this Isadore never comes?"

"I refuse to think negative thoughts. She must come." Sophia knew that Isadore's coming could spell the end to her own relationship with William.

Devere got up and strode to the door. "I understand how much you want to nullify this marriage, but equally as important is stopping Finkel from destroying more lives."

* * *

At least he'd had the good sense to take the rented coach today. For a day that had begun so promising, yesterday was clearly the worst day in his life. He'd thought he would never thaw. And he was still convinced he would never find a woman more to his liking than Isadore.

She was corrupt. She lacked fidelity. She lied. Even knowing what he knew now about her, he still hungered for the woman! She shared his taste in poetry. Everything in her bearing bespoke aristocracy. By God, the woman was lovely, and her very touch was debilitating!

He grew nervous when he reached his house. He couldn't allow himself to see her. If she tried to speak to him, he must steel himself to turn his back on her. He would only stay there long enough to change into clothes for dinner, dinner with his brother Adam at their club.

Drawing in a breath, he entered his home and mounted the stairs. When he reached the second floor he began to relax. Dare he hope Isadore had left? Dare he hope he would never again have to see her? The thought of never seeing her again, though, made him melancholy.

In his chambers, Thompson greeted him and offered him a letter.

William looked down at the feminine script. "Is it from Isadore?"

Thompson nodded solemnly.

He should throw it in the fire. Instead he asked Thompson to bring him Madeira, and he went to sit before the fire and find out what the she-devil had to say to him.

Dearest William,

I beg your forgiveness for not telling you I was married. The marriage was a grievous mistake which has cost me dearly. You must have guessed that the union between me and my husband was never consummated. You are the only man with whom I've ever lain.

No matter what the repercussions may be, I could never regret the night I spent in your arms.

It is impossible for me to convey the melancholy in which I am steeped. To be trapped in a marriage in which I want no part is all the more painful now that I have finally learned what it is to love a man.

~ Isadore

He sat for a long while afterward. Were he a woman, he would have wept. The woman might be a liar, but strangely—especially considering he'd only known her for a matter of days—he believed she had written the truth.

It was bitter consolation to know that she loved him. For he could never possess Lord Evers' wife. Even if theirs was not a *real* marriage.

$\mathcal{C}$hapter 11

She'd seen him enter the house. Throughout the day she had not left the window in her chamber. When he'd come, her heart caught. The very sight of him was enough to send her pulse racing. How manly he looked as he eschewed the footman's offer of an umbrella and hastened up the steps.

Thompson would give him her letter. Would he come to her after he read it? She sat in her chamber for a considerable period of time. Certainly long enough for him to climb to his chambers, read his post, and change into appropriate evening dress. Somewhere in that hour he must have read her letter. Or, she thought with a fissure to her heart, would he merely have thrown it in the fire?

Finally, she heard the door to his bedchamber close. Her heartbeat accelerated. She glanced into the mirror to assure herself she looked presentable whilst listening intently to each step upon the corridor. Her breath stilled in her chest, she moved to the door, trembling in anticipation.

He did not so much as pause but continued on the stairs.

She slivered open her door to assure herself the footsteps had belonged to him. She could not mistake his thick golden hair as he descended the stairs. A moment later the front door closed.

In the same way a wife of many years knows the nuances in her husband's voice, Sophia had known William was too noble to carry on with another man's wife. Nothing she could say would alter the fact she was a married woman. Nothing could mend the deep chasm between them.

She went to Dottie. "Could you find out if Thompson delivered my letter to Mr. Birmingham?"

"Allow me to write a note." The maid moved to her French escritoire and wrote a single sentence upon a small sheet of foolscap. With a smile upon her slender face, Dottie then left the room.

She returned a moment later, frowning. "Mr. Thompson says he did give the letter to Mr. Birmingham and that Mr. Birmingham read it. He said his master sat there for a long while afterward, looking gloomy. Then when Mr. Thompson helped him into his evening clothes, Mr. Birmingham was much quieter than normal, and Mr. Thompson said he was very irritable.

Sophia's humiliation was complete. There was no hope. No hope she could dissolve her marriage. No hope she could ever again know William's love. No hope for happiness the rest of her life. A raw void centered in her heart. If she lived to be a hundred, that aching void would never be filled. For only one man could ever fill it. At seven and twenty, her life was over. A bride jilted at the altar could not feel more despair than Sophia felt at that moment.

Eyeing Dottie, she sighed. "Since my romance has withered so utterly hopelessly, I do hope, dear Dot, that you've got good news to report on your own."

"I've been waiting all afternoon for you to ask."

Dottie's buoyant smile stretched all the way across her face. "We sat together, and he 'eld me hand. No fellow's 'eld me hand since I was twelve. Course he can't talk to me because I can't answer—or leastways, he *thinks* I can't answer."

Dottie's happiness took a bit of the sting away from Sophia's own moroseness. "It sounds like you're having a proper courtship."

"But if I were really and truly proper I wouldn't be alone in a coach with a man with no chaperone."

"I believe those rules of propriety apply to maidens significantly younger than you. By the time a woman's reached thirty, she should be able to serve as her own chaperone."

Dottie's eyes widened. "I was forty on me last birthday."

"I know that very well."

"That's right. You got me this pretty little gold ring." She looked from the delicate ring up at Sophia, her eyes shimmering with gratitude. "I never in me whole life had something so beautiful."

Sophia was touched. "It certainly looks as if the last half of your life is shaping up to be the best. You are fortunate that your affection is returned by the only man who's ever really held it."

"Aye, milady."

Sophia would take her consolation in Dottie's joy. She stood. "Since Mr. Birmingham's gone out, I will avail myself of his library." She had to copy the list of Finkie's wicked schemes.

If she couldn't have William she would at least help him crush the awful man she'd had the misfortune to wed.

* * *

The following morning she watched solemnly as William left the house just before noon. Because the rain had finally stopped, he wore riding clothes and left on his horse.

She set the candelabra on her windowsill.

Not five minutes later, her brother came. Had Devere been watching the house? He would not have come so early if he bore bad news. She raced down the stairs to greet him.

"Mr. Beresford," she said for the benefit of the butler, "how very good of you to come! Why do we not go into the library today?" She did not want William to hear of her entertaining gentlemen in her bedchamber. Even if he never spoke to her again, she could not bear it were he to think her a woman of depraved morals.

They strolled along the entry hall to the library. She closed the door snugly behind them and faced him with a broad smile upon her face. "You've come with good tidings!"

He gave her a coy look. "Since I was a lad, you've always been able to read me like you used to devour those Minerva novels."

She happily nodded. "Please say Rutherford has found a way out of my . . . " She could not say *marriage*. "My misalliance with Lord Finkel."

He shook his head solemnly. "Sorry, Soph, that's *not* my good news."

She had been thinking with her heart and not her head. The possibility of ever dissolving her disastrous marriage to Lord Finkel was close to nonexistent. Her face collapsed.

"Rutherford's less optimistic with each passing day."

That's exactly what her mind had been telling her. She nodded gravely. "Then you got the money?" There was no way he could possibly be carrying eighty thousand pounds on him.

"I did, but I mean to protect my investment. I've hired a pair of Bow Street runners to deliver it. The money has been put into a fairly large sized valise which I daresay your Isadore will not be able to lift. It's beastly heavy. One of the runners will stay on at Grosvenor Square to protect you and the money until you give it to the real Isadore."

"You've thought of everything." She had to own she had been worried about the burden of being responsible for the money until the transfer.

If Isadore had done anything like this before, she would know to bring her own guards. Now Sophia would no longer be looking for a lone woman.

"While we're in this room I want you to see Mr. Birmingham's ledger. I've copied it for you, too." They went to the large writing table. Morning light streamed onto it from the tall, velvet-draped window a few feet behind it. She opened the ledger, and the two of them peered at the notes.

"Good God! I remember that scandal about Lady Sandington!" Devere said. "Her husband banished her to Scotland after Smith's newspaper ran that story. I suppose when she could no longer meet Finkel's demands, he exposed her. And that kind of exposure is just the kind of thing Finkel needed to ensure his other victims would keep on paying him."

"It's shameful."

"I wonder why your Mr. Birmingham is so interested in Lord Finkel? This investigation was obviously done before you two were acquainted."

She shrugged. "If you'll look at the last two

entries. The first, Lord Livingston. If I recall correctly, his seat is in Yorkshire?"

"It is."

"Then the final entry is merely a woman's name and a church name in Yorkshire. The night I met Mr. Birmingham, he was traveling from Yorkshire. He said he'd been visiting his sister, but I believe he went there to further his inquiries about Lord Finkel."

Devere's brows lowered. "What can be Birmingham's interest?"

"The vile Lord Finkel must have destroyed someone Mr. Birmingham loves. It's hard for you to conceive, but in this short time in which Mr. Birmingham and I have been acquainted, I have come to know his character. He is a true gentleman. Not only that, he's the sort of man who will always put himself out for another's benefit. He jeopardized his own life to keep me from Finkie's armed men. When they found me the morning after . . . the wedding."

"Then I am indebted to him. I shall have to meet this paragon. Even if he engages in criminal activity."

"I can't allow you to meet him. Not now anyway."

There was a knock upon the library door, and Fenton stepped in. "Mr. Beresford? Some men here to see you."

Devere and Sophia went to the door, and her glance dropped from the two sturdily-built men in red vests to the paisley valise that was sitting at the top doorstep.

"Thank you, gentlemen," Devere said, bending down to lift the valise. "I'll carry this upstairs for my s- - - friend, Miss Door."

As the brother and sister climbed the stairs, Devere spoke under his breath. "I warned the runners not to refer to me as Lord Devere." The higher they climbed, the shorter his breath became. "This is devilishly heavy," he said, panting. "Did you get a look at the chaps?"

"I don't know. I suppose I did."

When they reached her room, he said, "One of them will always be lurking around the center of Grosvenor Square. If you ever need help, you must seek one of the runners."

"I'm very grateful to you."

* * *

He'd been avoiding his house night and day all because of that blasted Isadore. It really wasn't right. The sooner they exchanged the bullion, the better. As long as the woman slept beneath his roof, he couldn't be free of the torturing pain of knowing she was just steps away, knowing that even if she were wed to another, she loved him. That she was in love with him increased his pain tenfold. How difficult it had been not to rush to her once he'd read her wrenching letter.

Nothing could ever alter the fact she was married to a noble man. Evers did not deserve to be a cuckold.

With firm resolve, William returned to his house that afternoon. Certain matters of business must be attended to in his library. If he saw Isadore, he would not speak. Surely by now she had discovered he was inflexible about his resolve not to renew their . . . *affair* was too sordid a word for what had occurred between Isadore and him that night.

Lovemaking. His mouth went dry. Melancholy seeped into every pore in his body.

As much as he still longed for her, he would ignore her persistent tug at his heart. He would ignore his own throbbing need. By omission, he would take the first steps to healing.

When he finally entered his home that afternoon, he strode straight to the library. As soon as he entered the chamber, he smelled roses. Her scent. His heartbeat accelerated. Then she stood. She'd been seated on the sofa near the fire, a book in her lap. Her huge dark eyes were incredibly solemn. "Hello, William."

He hadn't wanted to see her. But now he drank his fill of her loveliness. Today she wore a pure white day dress and looked as if she'd fallen from the heavens. The white brought out the white in her eyes and matched her perfect teeth. It was stunning with her deep brown hair and dark eyes.

As unconsciously as breathing, his gaze swept over her. From the spiral of her curls to her bare, milky shoulders to the smoothly rounded tops of her breasts, he looked. She was perfection.

He could not deny he was mad with love of her. And, God, but he wanted her!

Like a sheet of foolscap thrown on fire, his resolve was destroyed. "Good day, madam." He tried to sound stiff as he strolled to his writing table.

She remained standing. "May I ask you a question? It does not pertain to me, and I give you my word your response will be held in the strictest of confidence."

"Very well. One question and one question only, then I must ask you to leave my library."

A hurt look swept across her face.

He was not unaffected. It had pained him to hear his own words.

"I'm sorry there have been lies between us," she said. "I seem to make a habit of doing things the wrong way. I confess that whilst in this chamber sitting where you're sitting right now, I opened your ledger."

His anger flared and he swore beneath his breath. "You had no right!" Information in that ledger could destroy people's lives. He should have guarded it better. He recalled that she had just used the words *held in the strictest confidence.* In spite of her catalogue of wrong-doing, he believed that she would not use the information in that ledger for nefarious purposes.

She nodded ruefully. "I know. You see, I'm a hopeless rule breaker." She took a couple of steps closer. "I should like to know why you want to destroy the vile Lord Finkel."

It was several moments before he could answer. Her question had taken him by complete surprise. The fact she'd used the word *vile* indicated she must know something of the man's evildoings. "I will not answer that question until you answer mine."

Their eyes locked.

"What question would that be?" she asked.

"Do *you* wish to see Lord Finkel destroyed?"

"More than anything."

"Then I will not deny that is my desire. I won't rest until he's ruined. He destroyed the life of my closest friend."

She nodded. "It is because of his threats to ruin my sister that I entered into my calamitous union. I should like to help you ruin him in any way I can."

"I've spent four years trying to gather information against him."

"I wish you'd tell me about your friend," she said in a soft voice.

He was powerless to deny her. He moved to the fire and watched the dancing flames while gathering his thoughts. She came to stand beside him, all softness and smelling of roses, and he thought his heart could burst with love of her. A love he would never acknowledge.

"David Balderstone was one of the nicest persons I've ever known. I met him when I was eight. I was new at Eton and enormously homesick and scared, and—already having a year there under his belt—he took me under his wing and showed me great kindness. We became great friends, lifelong friends. He told me things he told no one else.

"That's how I learned about his compulsive attraction to his elder brother's wife. Her marriage was not a particularly happy one, and because his brother was many years older, Stoney—that's what we called David—wasn't particularly close to him.

"The attraction turned to something much deeper. Finkel somehow found out about it and threatened to tell his brother. Stoney gave Finkel every farthing he possessed. But Finkel wanted more. Stoney then came to me for a loan. I knew it would never be repaid, but that didn't matter. It was the first time in our long friendship Stoney had ever asked me for money, even though I was much wealthier than him. He had grown thinner. He was distraught. He had severed the relationship with the woman he loved if not wisely, most passionately. I was worried about him.

"I didn't hear from him for weeks. I grew concerned and went to his lodgings." William drew in a deep breath. Even after four years it was still painful to recall that day. "Stoney killed himself with a razor to his throat." William's voice broke.

Isadore moved closer to him and set a gentle hand to his shoulder.

He gathered his composure. "He left a letter for me. He was too proud to keep coming to me for money. In his desperation, he thought killing himself was the only way to protect the woman he loved. There was also the shame of ever having to face his brother."

"The poor, poor man," she murmured. "Finkel's depraved. We must stop him."

"The pity of it is none of those I've talked to will publicly denounce him. I can't even tell the magistrates about Stoney's plight without violating his last wishes."

"There's no one on the list who would testify against him?"

He shook his head sadly. His eyes met hers again. "I don't suppose you—or your sister—would?"

"My sister's still a maiden. It would ruin her."

Something within him sagged.

"I . . . could testify about the vile man's threats and schemes with me, but I could never mention my sister's name."

"In a case like this, a preponderance of evidence would be most helpful. It would also be helpful to have someone from the aristocracy speak of his ill deeds. What would be most helpful of all would be to find something in Finkel's own hand which would reveal his evil scheming. Did you, perchance, save the blackmail notes you received?"

She shook her head. "I burned them."

"A pity."

"A person I know well—an aristocrat actually—is acquainted with at least one name on your list. I will see if he can encourage that person to speak against Lord Finkel."

Her husband. No, not her husband. Her husband must unknowingly be allies with Finkel. William could never believe Lord Evers of being in league with a blackmailer. Not one word had ever been uttered against Lord Evers' integrity. And William's own experiences with the ambassador reinforced his high opinion of Evers' honesty. He had once declined a bribe from William. No government official in any capital had ever refused to be beholden to the powerful Birmingham family. Except for the noble Lord Evers.

How peculiar it was to be standing here with the man's wife.

Especially after William had vowed he'd not speak with the woman. Yet here he was spilling details of private matters he'd never told anyone other than his brothers. He turned to her and did his best to appear icy. "That would be very good, madam." Stiffly, he returned to his desk. "Any word on the bullion?"

"Any day now."

He avoided eye contact with her, merely nodding as he opened a drawer and tried to appear as if he were searching for something.

She knew she'd been dismissed.

From beneath hooded eyes, he watched her go. How elegantly she moved. What a fool he was to be so obsessed with her. Would she ever lose her vast appeal?

She might be a liar, a criminal, and another man's wife, but William could take painful consolation that he was the only man she'd ever given herself to.

Her letter had not been a lie.

$\mathcal{C}$hapter 12

As had become her constant custom, Sophia was sitting before her window looking out over Grosvenor Square the following morning. She'd allowed herself to hope that after breaking the ice the previous night in his library, William might thaw. Perhaps he would come to her this morning and not be that icy stranger who had so curtly dismissed her the night before.

But that was not to be. She watched with a sinking feeling as he left the house just before noon. He had not tried to utter a single word to her. He had not wanted to see her at all.

She'd once more been thinking with her heart and not her head. Nothing had thawed since he'd spoken his final chilling words.

After his horse pulled away, she set the candelabra in her window. Perhaps her brother might come. Even though she knew that dissolving her marriage was hopeless, she continued to hope Devere's solicitor had found a way.

To be pragmatic, she dispatched Dottie and Thompson to Curzon Street once more. They would walk today since it was not raining. That would give them more time together, Sophia thought affectionately.

She only prayed that Dottie would not forget and start talking.

As Sophia had lain awake in her bed, unable to sleep, she realized she had to do whatever she could to bring Finkie to justice. She and William working together was far better than either of them working alone.

His ledger had provided her with a lead. A man acquainted with her brother.

Her brother arrived in Grosvenor Square at noon. As she saw him approach on horseback, she rushed to Dottie and asked that she relieve her at the window. "Come to the library at once and let me know if you see any woman who might be Isadore," Sophia instructed.

In the library, Sophia greeted her brother.

"What is it now?" he asked impatiently.

"Lord Finkel must be stopped."

"I agree."

"You are acquainted with Sir George Malvern, are you not?"

He raised a brow. "I am."

She strode to William's ledger and opened it. "We know from Mr. Birmingham's book Sir George is one of Finkie's victims. What we need is someone like Sir George to be willing to come forward with accusations of Lord Finkel's evil deeds. Mr. Birmingham wasn't able to persuade him, but I think I can. Everyone respects you."

His eyes narrowed suspiciously. "What are you proposing?"

"For you and me to pay him a visit. We must appeal to his compassion for others who've been injured by Finkie."

"What makes you think he'll agree for us when he's already turned down your Mr. Birmingham?"

She recalled the names in William's ledger. Sir George's recently deceased son was one of Finkie's victims. "I shall first point out the person he wished most to protect from exposure is now dead. Secondly, you will assure him that he'll be doing what's right, that he'll save many, many people from Lord Finkel's treacherous clutches."

"It's not as if I really know Sir George. I merely nod to him from time to time at White's."

"But, my dear brother, you outrank almost everyone at White's. Everyone curries your favor and is flattered by your attentions."

Devere did not protest.

Her brother was inherently honest. He could not deny that his sister spoke the truth.

"Very well. I'll send around a note asking to see him on a private matter Wednesday afternoon. Can you meet me at his house on Half Moon Street then?"

"I will."

* * *

As William made his way home from visiting Adam, the skies erupted. He was in for another drenching. A pity he hadn't taken the coach. When given the choice, he always preferred to ride Thunder. Being on horseback made whipping in and out of London's snarled conveyances a great deal faster. On a cold, damp day like today, though, exposing himself like this was sheer lunacy. Especially given his state of ill health.

He'd had a miserable night sleeping—and not just because Isadore haunted his thoughts. He would go to sleep only to be awakened by a coughing fit. When he had finally awakened for good, it hurt to swallow. His throat felt as if it had been ignited by a torch.

He could have lain in bed all day, but he refused to. It was far too painful to be in the same house with Isadore. How difficult it had been to be in the same room with her last night and know he could not act upon the strumming desire he was incapable of suppressing.

But now he had no choice. His bloody bed beckoned. He felt wretched. The stinging rain wasn't helping matters. It drilled into him, through his woolen pants, its chill penetrating to his very bones.

He dismounted in front of his house, handing his horse off to a footman, and inside, handing his dripping greatcoat off to Fenton. Climbing the stairs was an effort. He felt so bloody bad.

When he reached his chambers, Thompson greeted him. "It appears the master has once again experienced a thorough soaking. Come, we must get you out of those wet clothes!"

William collapsed into a chair. "Be a good man and help me out of my boots."

Thompson stooped down and began to tug. "Your voice sounds awful."

"I feel awful."

"What you need is a warm bed."

"Excellent advice."

Thompson's eyes rounded. "I've never known you to lie abed in the daytime in all these years I've been serving you."

"That's because I haven't been sick in all these years you've been serving me."

After the boots were removed, Thompson stood. William stumbled to his feet, peeled off his soaked clothing, and climbed into bed.

"Allow me to close the draperies so the room will be dark," Thompson said. "What you need is a good sleep."

* * *

Sophia had seen him enter. The poor man looked like a drowned pup. She heard him pass her door when he went to his chamber. When she heard footsteps on the corridor fifteen minutes later, she opened her door, hoping to see William. But it was not William. It was Thompson.

She pushed aside her initial disappointment and called out to the valet.

He stopped and turned. "Yes, Miss Door?"

"Do you know if your master is dining at home tonight?" What business was it of hers to be asking such a question? She prayed William was planning to so that she could join him.

A sad look came over his face. "I couldn't say, Miss. Mr. Birmingham has come down with a nasty chill. He's in bed now—a first for my master."

Her face turned sad. Twice now—three times if one counted their miserable journey to London— he had foolishly exposed himself to the brutal cold and punishing rain. She felt responsible. Had William not been so angry with her he wouldn't have acted so foolishly. She was even responsible for the destruction of his carriage that had made their drive to London so uncomfortable. (Of course, if one were laying blame where blame belonged, Finkie was actually responsible.)

A pity she'd brought her own grief upon dear William Birmingham. If something happened to him, she truly would enter a convent and spend the rest of her days eschewing her riches, repenting her sins, and helping lepers. Isn't that the sort of thing one did in a convent? She wondered if convents permitted Anglicans. She really didn't know anything at all about convents.

"Oh, the poor, dear man!" said she. "I must

hasten down and ask that the cook make soup for the master."

* * *

He'd been dreaming that he was trudging, half clothed, through fields of snow. He was bitterly cold. When he awakened he realized it was the damn cold in his bedchamber that had cut short his slumber. Neither a blazing fire nor a pile of blankets could compensate for the damp chill which permeated the room.

He looked at the clock upon his mantel to discover he'd slept for more than two hours.

He'd thought he would awaken and feel his old self, but he still did not feel quite the thing. He didn't actually have a fever. He just felt like his head might explode. And he was beginning to think he would never again be warm.

By the time he had fully separated dream from reality, a knock sounded upon his door. He'd sent hovering Thompson away hours before. "Who is it?" He was surprised at the hoarseness of his voice.

The door inched open, and Isadore stood there holding a bed tray. She had apparently enlisted her sister to do the door duties because her own hands were otherwise occupied. She dismissed the poor mute, then turned all her attention—and a most angelic smile—upon him. "I had Cook make you some fresh lentil soup. My nurse used to swear that highly seasoned lentil soup warded off the most offensive cases of lung fever. She always insisted that we have lentil soup at the first sign of a chill, and we were all remarkably healthy."

So he'd been right about her being gently bred. Only the wealthy and the nobles employed nurses to raise their children. But, then, Lord Evers would hardly be marrying a woman from a lower station.

She wore white again and looked far too ethereal and far too flawless to be a mortal. He was mesmerized by her loveliness as she gracefully moved toward him. The white was a stunning backdrop for her luxurious dark brown locks.

As she came closer, his breathing accelerated. He wished to God she didn't have such an effect upon him, wished to God he could be impervious to her.

Bloody hell. He'd have to sit up now, but he couldn't do so while she was in the room. He hadn't a stitch on. And, besides, the prospect of leaving the warmth of his blankets was not pleasant.

"I will own," he croaked in his compromised voice, "my throat craves something hot, and I cannot deny that I'm hungry."

"You sound terrible!" Her gaze went to his bare shoulders and froze.

His breath grew even more labored.

She recovered promptly. "Direct me to where I can find you a night shirt. You must be freezing in this chilly room. I don't know why your house is always so beastly cold."

His misery was stronger than his desire to appear unaffected by the cold. "Look in the linen press."

She set the tray down on his writing desk and went to the apple green, Chinoiserie-style press, withdrew a heavy twill night shirt, and brought it to him.

His brows lowered. "You shouldn't be here."

She started to giggle.

"What do you find to laugh about?"

"Can you be saying it's improper for me to see your bare shoulders?" She laughed some more.

"It's not proper!"

"Have you forgotten that I've seen every inch of you beneath the glow of firelight?" She spoke in a velvety timbre.

Never mind that he was sick man, he was instantly aroused.

But he had vowed never to act on his desire for her. She was Lord Evers' wife.

"That was before I knew you were married to another man," he grumbled. "Turn around whilst I put on my shirt."

She giggled some more as she faced away from him.

He eased from beneath his warm covers in much the same way one eases into a frigid lake on a warm day. Damn! His room was bloody cold. He threw on the nightshirt, which did offer a modicum of warmth. Then he launched into a coughing fit.

"I know it's beastly cold in this chamber," she said, "but the soup will help to warm you."

He looked up at her—or, rather, at her back. "You can turn around now."

She lifted the tray and came to him.

"What else do you have on the tray?" he asked.

"Before I tell you, I have something to say."

He glared, trying to appear as if he were completely unaffected by her. Though he was anything but.

"I know you're angry with me, and you have every right to be, but as long as we're waiting for the bullion, as long as you're kind enough to permit me to stay here, can we at least act friendly to one another?"

She sighed and her voice softened. "I know there can't be anything more between us, but please don't completely slam the door on me. I couldn't bear it. Can we not be friends?" Those huge dark eyes of her were incredibly sorrowful when she looked at him.

He must be bewitched. Though he'd somehow managed to deny himself what he wanted most, he seemed incapable of denying her anything else. He had permitted her to continue on at Grosvenor Square. And now he was agreeing to feign friendship with her when with every breath he drew he wanted so much more. He solemnly nodded.

A smile lifted her beautiful face. "Good." She set the tray in front of him. "I've also brought you a decoction of lungwort to help you feel better. My old nurse- - -"

"Swore by its effectiveness."

She laughed. "What a pity it is, Mr. Birmingham, that you are so easily anticipating my sentences. I must be as dull as Hannah More."

"I thought all women admired Hannah More."

"Simple minded women who are exceedingly pious. I hardly fit that description."

His thoughts exactly. He'd rather undergo a bloodletting than read one of the More woman's didactic tracts. "It appears there's another area in which we are in perfect agreement, Miss Door."

He had suffered a flinch of disappointment when she'd addressed him by his surname. It was better this way, though. It was better not to recall a night when a lady he'd called Isadore offered a woman's most precious gift to a man she called

William.

He still couldn't shake those memories from his mind. He *had* been her first. It would have been so much easier now, so much less painful, had he not been!

"And I brought this," she said, smiling as she held up a volume of Pope's poems. "As you did to me when I was infirm, I shall read to you. I shouldn't like for you to leave your bed until I can verify that your good health has been restored."

She remembered how much he admired Pope. "You must have been a firstborn," he muttered with mock indignation.

Her dark eyes danced. "Are you saying that I am accustomed to ordering about a pack of younger siblings?"

"I am."

A look of concentration crossed her face. "I was *not* the first born. I have an elder brother, but I was the first daughter, and I regret to admit that I was rather authoritarian with my younger siblings—and still am."

"I rest my case."

She moved closer. Her light rose scent affected him almost as profoundly as her reminder that she'd seen every inch of his flesh beneath candlelight. "I would rather you drink your lungwort. It's preferable, I am told, if one takes medicinals along with food."

"Miss Door, you might call a bowl of lentil soup food, but I most certainly do not."

Her laughter once again rang out.

A woman who laughed. He could only plight his life to a woman with an excellent sense of humor. How it tortured him to know the one woman with whom he was perfectly compatible was already wed. William had never before been a jealous man. Until now. As honorable as Lord Evers was, William was beginning to loathe him.

"Spoken like a man."

"I am a man."

Her long, dark lashes lowered, and her voice went husky. "Yes, I know."

Dear God, give me strength. To get his thoughts away from the dangerous trajectory they'd taken, he grabbed the decoction of lungwort and gulped it down. "Why in the blazes did you not tell me how foul tasting it was?"

"Because I suspected you'd be like my youngest brother and refuse to imbibe."

"Ah ha! Now I know the source of your propensity to lie! I can see you telling an innocent little lad that a decoction of slimy lungwort tastes as good as plum pudding."

Her response was another laugh. "Really, Mr. Birmingham, it is vastly UNgallant of you to continue referring to my falsehoods. A gentleman simply doesn't do such."

Yesterday he would never have dreamed that he could be laughing over the many ways she had duped him. As much as he wanted to dislike her, he could not. In fact, he was happy she had come to brighten what had been a miserable day.

He started on his soup. It felt soothing on his raw throat. After three or four spoonfuls, he was warming. "Thank you, Miss Door, and thanks to your old nurse. The soup is the very thing. I'm feeling much better."

She still stood beside his bed, and now she came closer and pressed a gentle hand to his forehead. "Thank God you don't have a fever."

He could not deny that she'd been concerned

over him. How much less agonizing it would have been if she had no feelings for him whatsoever.

As he was finishing his soup, she took the slender chair from in front of his desk, brought it to his bedside, and sat. "Before I begin reading, should you like more soup?"

He shook his head. "For something that is *not* food, it was rather filling."

They both laughed.

"I wish I could make this room warmer for you," she said. "I think it's a matter of the excessive cold outside. It's now snowing, you know."

"Good thing I wasn't riding when that started."

"You shouldn't have been riding anything in this nasty cold!"

"Spoken like the firstborn daughter."

It was funny how they knew little things about one another but knew so little of the whole picture. He knew enough to know that if she hadn't been married, he would have raced her to the alter less than a week after they met. It was a source of almost unimaginable pain that what had started out so sublimely had ended so cruelly.

"Are you ready for me to read to you?"

He nodded.

Her voice was lovely, even melodic, as she read. His lids began to droop. The last words he heard were *not proud Olympus yields a nobler sight.*

$\mathcal{C}$hapter 13

At the time she calculated he normally awakened—judging from the time he left his chambers each day—she brought a breakfast tray to his room. Once again, Dottie knocked upon and opened the door, and then Sophia strolled in, a bright smile on her face.

She'd actually been smiling quite a bit since she'd walked into this same chamber eighteen hours earlier. Even as she had lain in bed pondering the hopelessness of her marital situation, she smiled because she and William were friends again. She smiled because they could laugh together. She smiled because as long as she was permitted to stay at his house, she could be with him. She valued these moments all the more after the days of their estrangement—and because these moments would be taken away far too soon.

Her gaze connected with his. There was a flash of some emotion in his mossy eyes as they lazily traveled the length of her. He was sitting up in bed, still in his snowy white nightshirt. How rugged he looked with a day's growth of beard.

She hadn't been prepared for the effect it would have upon her to see him when he awakened in the morning. Memories of that other morning flooded her. How she wanted to climb in that bed with him and feel her flesh pressed to his. Her breath sputtered in her chest like a kettle about to boil.

Perhaps if the draperies were opened her mind would not be reverting to those nocturnal memories. She gathered her wits. "How are you feeling this morning?"

"Not good," he said in a nasal tone.

She moved to the bed, set down the tray, and began to pour his chamomile tea into an eggshell-thin porcelain cup rimmed in gilt. "My old nurse said chamomile tea is the best thing to open up the stuffy head in the morning."

"And we know your old nurse was always right."

Even as she nodded, her brows squeezed together as she regarded him. His croaking voice sounded terrible. "I had so hoped you'd be better this morning, but Nurse used to say that when the head is clogged, it's always worst in the morning. Then once one is sitting up and can expel the clogging, one can commence to feeling better."

"I do hope your old nurse is right about this."

"You sound awful."

"You look beautiful."

She was completely taken aback by his compliment. For a moment she wondered how she should respond, then she decided a simple, "Thank you," would do.

"I must tell you I'm impervious to beautiful, *married* females," he said.

"Yes, I know."

He sipped his tea, then favored her with a smile. "Nothing could have felt better on my throat. Thank you."

"I thought perhaps porridge would give you some nourishment while soothing your throat, too."

His eyes danced. "How well your old nurse taught you."

She moved away and began to open the crimson draperies at all three of his windows. "That's better. Look if you will, Mr. Birmingham, at how sunny it is today."

"But it's still icy cold."

"Indeed it is. When I looked out my window this morning, there was frost on all the rooftops." Her attention turned to his fire. It looked as if it had freshly been built. "Did the charwoman awaken you?"

He started to answer, but began to cough. A hacking cough. Finally, he said, "No. My body awakens at the same time every day no matter how little sleep I've had."

Her brows lowered. "Did you sleep poorly?"

"Actually, I slept quite well. I woke up once coughing but had no difficulty going back to sleep. The melodious tones of Miss Door reciting my favorite Poet must have acted as a sedative."

The chair she'd pulled beside his bed last night was still there. She sat in it. "Do you know, Mr. Birmingham, I believe you favor Pope because he satirizes everything. I believe you're very cynical yourself."

He smiled. "I shall take that as a compliment."

"See! Nurse was right! Your voice is already better."

"Then I shall be most indebted to your old nurse."

She sighed. "It is such a pity that you're not an upstanding citizen, Mr. Birmingham."

His brows lowered. "Why do you say that?"

"Because if you were, you could command the

respect needed to sway members of the House of Lords."

"That's right. Lord Finkel would have to be tried by his peers in the House of Lords."

"If only you were an aristocrat. An aristocrat wouldn't even have to go into the lurid details about Stoney's sister-in-law. Other lords would be satisfied if a respected lord said *a friend* and did not have to name Stoney."

"But as you say, I'm neither an aristocrat nor am I respectable."

The more she was with him, the more difficult it was for her to think him disreputable. He possessed too many fine attributes.

His gaze went to the door on the other side of his chamber. She suspected it was the door to his dressing room. "I wonder why Thompson hasn't been in this morning?" he asked.

"I asked him to let you sleep."

"Yet you were willing to wake me?"

"Not before a time when I thought you were accustomed to waking."

A knock sounded upon his door, and after William responded, Fenton opened the door.

"Miss Isadore Door has a visitor."

Oh dear. She'd told Devere not to ever come if William was at home.

"A man?" William barked.

"No, Mr. Birmingham. A young woman."

Her first thought was that it was Isadore. But Isadore would not be asking for Sophia. She knew nothing of Sophia's existence. Isadore would be seeking William.

Puzzled, Sophia stood.

* * *

All the way down the stairs, Sophia was

perplexed. No one knew she was here, except for her brother. He was the only one who would have known what ridiculous name she was assuming, and the caller had obviously asked to see Miss Isadore Door. Just before Sophia reached the library, she had worked out who her caller must be.

She cautiously opened the door and quietly shut it behind her just before she came face to face with her *real* sister. The two stood staring at one another for a moment.

No one witnessing the scene would ever believe these two females were sisters. This blonde looked nothing like Sophia or Devere, both of whom were possessed of dark hair and even darker eyes. This young woman's eyes were fair, like a pale blue translucent sky. She was also considerably younger than Sophia. Where Sophia's first Season was a distant memory, this lady looked as if she had just reached the age of coming out.

She flew into Sophia's arms. "Ever since Devere told me how that odious Lord Finkel forced you to marry him, I've felt as if I could throw myself from the top of St. Paul's."

Sophia held her at arm's length and peered into her misty eyes. "I beg that you put away such morbid thoughts. Your death would be a thousand times worse than kissing Lord Finkel— though I will own kissing Lord Finkel was vastly unpleasant!"

Maryann swiped away a tear, and the two sisters giggled.

"I'm happy you got away from him."

"My success at that remains to be seen. Come, pet, let's move closer to the fire. This house has abominable drafts." This room was just as chilly as William's.

The two sat on a sofa in front of the fire.

"I want to do anything I can to help set you free from Lord Finkel. I mean to tell the magistrates about the threats, about my . . . my indiscretion."

"And have it published in the newspapers?"

Maryann sat up straighter and spoke with defiance. "If need be."

Sophia regarded her from beneath lowered brows. "Have you spoken of this to Devere?"

Maryann's bravado wilted, and she shook her head. "It was mortifying enough when he confronted me about that disastrous deed I committed when I was fifteen. I have never known such embarrassment. My brother speaking to me about such an intimate occurrence! I was incapable of looking him in the eye."

"I can speak for Devere when I say he would never permit you to bring down such a scandal upon our house." Sophia knew spoiling Maryann's reputation and the subsequent absence of marital prospects would worry Devere far worse than a scandal touching the family, but she wanted her sister to think that publicizing her confession would hurt the whole family. Obviously, Maryann, in her desire to make amends, had completely disregarded herself. "You must also be cognizant that no man would ever offer for you if you are known to have *ruined* yourself. Don't you want to marry?"

Tears began to trickle down Maryann's cheeks. "I gave up the right to hope for that."

Sophia clasped her sister's hands. "Don't ever think that. Look at you! You're beautiful. You will have all the gentlemen begging for your hand."

Maryann shook her head. "But I cannot marry!

How could I enter a marriage without being truthful?"

"Honesty is highly overrated. Often the truth hurts innocent people."

"But a man would know about those things. He would know he wasn't my first."

"Men aren't as knowledgeable as you would give them credit for. And you must consider, you only did it once! That would hardly make you an old hand at that sort of thing. I daresay you could easily pass yourself off as quite an innocent."

The younger sister started to cry. "Devere said you hadn't . . . hadn't done the deed with Lord Finkel, but you seem awfully knowledgeable about these things." She started crying so hard she could hardly talk, but she kept trying to get the sputtering words out. "I'm so sorry. If I had to . . . to be with that odious Lord Finkel I *would* pitch myself off the top of St. Paul's."

"If you don't quit invoking St. Paul's I'll demand that Devere send you back to Hamberly!" Sophia cringed. "Such an ugly way to go. One's whole body would be crushed into pieces, and I suspect there would be an inordinate amount of blood. If I were going to do away with myself, I'd want to choose something that wouldn't disfigure."

"Like poison?"

"I don't know. I've been told some poisons make one cast up all their accounts before they die. I shouldn't want anyone to find my dead body in a nasty pool like that."

Maryann nodded. "There is that."

"Enough gruesome talk."

"You have done the deed, have you not?" Maryann asked.

Sophia nodded sheepishly.

"Oh, no! It's all my fault!" she began to wail.

"Not with Finkie."

The younger sister's head snapped upward. She looked at Sophia as if she'd just sprouted a second head. "Then I'm not the cause of your . . . "

"No, you're not. It didn't happen until *after* I left Finkie."

Now Maryann's eyes rounded. "With Mr. Birmingham!"

A dreamy look came over Sophia's face as she nodded.

"What a horrible man! Devere will want to kill him."

"He's not a horrible man," Sophia said, her voice soft. "He asked me to marry him. Before he learned that I was already wed. Or actually, that Isadore is wed. Though, of course, I am too." Now she felt like wailing.

"Devere told me about how you came to be Isadore. Has the real Isadore shown up?"

"Not yet."

"How can I help you?"

Sophia's thoughts flitted through her brain like leaves scattering on the winds. "I can't always be watching for Isadore. Dottie's been spelling me when I can't sit and watch, but I would prefer you."

"I will. How will you explain my presence to Mr. Birmingham?"

Sophia thought on it for a moment. Nothing ever popped into her heard without her making a concentrated effort. Finally, she came up with the explanation. "We will give the partial truth. I will say you're my sister. But of course you'll have to use a different name."

"You're going to want me to be a Door." She did

not look happy.

"Yes. You're to be Theodora Door."

Maryann rolled her eyes. "Next you'll be saying we have a brother named Dorian."

"I already have."

* * *

When she returned to William's chamber, he was fully dressed and seated at his desk perusing the day's post. She stood at the open door, gawking. He looked as if he'd had a complete recovery, which made her joyous. On the other hand, it saddened her to know that were he well, he would no longer need her. She'd have no reason to come to his bedchamber, nor would she be permitted to softly read poetry to him.

He smiled up at her. "I owe my thanks to you and to your former nurse. The chamomile tea and porridge were exactly what I needed." His voice, while still hoarse, has lost the nasal tone which sounded like someone speaking from down in a well.

"I do hope your illness is behind you."

He set down his pen. "So are you going to tell me who your female caller was?"

"Of course."

"I can depend upon you to tell me the version you prefer to tell me without regard to its veracity."

"Of course."

"So?"

"My younger sister came."

"Another sister? Is this one deaf?"

"No. She's a lovely young lady who happens to miss me most profoundly. I do hope you don't mind that I've asked her to stay with me for a few days. She won't be any trouble. She'll share my chamber as we did when we were younger."

"It's nothing to me if she stays. And what is this sister's name?"

"Theodora."

His eyes flashed with mirth. "Theodora Door?"

"Indeed." She drew a breath. "I do hope that just because you're feeling better you are not going out in this wretched cold."

"I have decided to stay in today." He stood. "And now that you've finished speaking to your *sister* in the library, I have correspondence that demands my attention."

"I'll come with you. There's a matter I wish to discuss."

As they descended the stairs, she reiterated how delighted she was that he was showing such improvement. "I daresay if you were foolish enough to go out, you'd pay dearly with a dangerous setback."

In the library, he sat at his long writing table, and she returned to the sofa. "It's much colder by that window," she said. "Perhaps you should come closer to the fire. I don't know why your house is so dreadfully cold."

"I've got on a warm coat."

"Just walking beside that writing table, I get chilled."

His heavy-lidded eye flicked to her. "That's because you're dressed in much too flimsy a fashion."

"How peculiar I would look were I to walk about your house in my velvet cloak. Even if it hadn't been dirtied and torn on the night of . . . the night we met at the Prickly Pig."

"What is it you wanted to speak to me about."

"Lord Finkel."

He regarded her with a quizzing look. "I've been meaning to ask if you know him personally."

"I do. Because of my familiarity with his habits, I've thought of something that might help us get information to use against him."

"You've piqued my interest."

"It will take a lot of courage, but I have no doubts courage is a trait you possess in abundance."

The way his eyes flashed, the way he sat there with so commanding a presence, it was difficult to believe his health had been compromised. "I am gratified that you think so," he said.

"I propose that we sneak inside of Lord Finkel's house when I'm sure he'll be elsewhere. We could be at liberty to search for incriminating evidence to use against him. Things like the original letters he's using to blackmail his victims."

His eyes narrowed. "What do you mean *we*? That most certainly does *not* sound like a mission upon which I would permit a woman to come. It could be very dangerous."

She could tell from his response that such a mission appealed to her fearless lover.

"But I not only know his habits, I also know his house." Her voice softened. "I could never be scared as long as you were with me."

"Madam, your trust in my abilities is vastly overrated."

A smile on her earnest face, she shrugged.

"Have you thought this out?"

"I have."

"You might know about Finkel, but what of his servants? He must have many."

"He does."

"Then how in the devil are *we* to search his

house?"

"Close to midnight every Thursday he goes to Mrs. Garth's establishment and plays faro and other games of chance until morning light."

"While his servants sleep," he said in a thoughtful voice. "I see what you're getting at, but a man with as many enemies as Finkel is sure to have his door locked and bolted."

"I leave it to you to figure out that part. There is the fact that you're very wealthy. Perhaps you could devise a way to bribe a servant."

He pursed his lips in thought. "That just might work. I can send Thompson along to make contact with the servants."

He looked down at the pile of letters and tradesmen's bills he'd brought along. "Shall we plan for this Thursday?"

She nodded. "I suppose it will actually be Friday by the time we get into his house." She stood and went to leave the room. Now that they had patched up their frail relationship, she didn't want her presence to be annoying. He clearly wished to work on his correspondence. Alone.

"By the way, when do I get to meet Miss Theodora Door?" he asked.

"Today if you like."

He drew a breath. "Perhaps at dinner. I shall dine in tonight."

$\mathcal{C}$hapter 14

Regardless of whether he owed his recovery to Isadore or to her childhood nurse, William was grateful for the improvement. He'd seldom felt worse than on the previous afternoon when, like a fool, he'd once again been caught in icy rain. With each step of his horse back to Grosvenor Square he had thought of how miserable he felt and how comforting a warm bed would be. He must have been very sick because William never slept in the daytime.

Even this morning the effects of his illness had lingered, but now as he spent the afternoon in his library, it occurred to him that while he was not experiencing a complete recovery, he did show vast improvement. The fact that he was dressed and out of his bed was proof. He could not have climbed from his bed four and twenty hours earlier.

As he spent the afternoon in his library, he was unable to repress the bittersweet memory of Isadore's soft voice as she had read Pope to him the previous night. The listening had brought him joy. Until he remembered that she belonged to another man.

Even now it seemed that her rose scent lingered in the library. Why did this woman affect him so profoundly? After several starts and stops on his correspondence, he put down his pen. It was no use attempting to write an amusing letter to his brother-in-law when his every thought was on Isadore. He cursed himself for a coward. Had he not sworn not to speak to her, not to be civil to her? Yet he'd weakened at her concern for him.

The woman might be a liar, a no-good smuggler, and an unfaithful wife, but he knew she had not feigned her worry over him. Was he more the fool to believe the wrenching words she'd written in that solitary letter?

The longer he sat at the writing table, the colder he became. She had been right about that too. It was much cooler near the window. It wouldn't do for him to have a setback. He was far too active to be forced back to bed. He went and sat on the sofa near the fire. And her scent was even stronger there.

He pictured her in the thin muslin dress of soft coral and remembered about her tattered cloak. Was that why she was not dressed more warmly? An idea struck him, and he got up and rang for a servant.

Fenton came.

William unlocked a desk drawer and picked up a small pouch of coins. "I wish you to send one of the footmen to Conduit Street to purchase a velvet cloak for Miss Isadore Door and see that she gets it before dinner." He tossed the money. "This should cover it."

* * *

"I beg that you say as little as possible," Sophia said to Maryann. The two ladies, along with Sophia's maid, had all dressed in finery for dinner. Though she knew of no one who had ever worn a velvet cloak in the dining chamber, she chose to do so tonight. She wished to show William how much she cherished his thoughtful gesture in purchasing it to replace the one she'd ruined climbing out her window at Finkie's that night.

Besides, the cloak's warmth would be most welcome in this chilly house.

Maryann effected a haughty look. "I have no intentions of being anything more than passably civil to the man who corrupted my sister. And, furthermore, I do not socialize with smugglers."

"Nothing is ever all black or all white, my dear sister. Withhold judgment on Mr. Birmingham until you meet him." What female would not fall hopelessly in love with him? His absence of rank or pedigree mattered not. There wasn't a man in the kingdom who was William's equal.

Dottie nodded emphatically at the younger sister. "While ye normally can't trust yer sister's selection in men, I'm telling you this man was put on this earth for Lady Sophia. You'll see fer yerself. He be a real gentlemen—in spite of his occupation."

Sophia put an index finger to her lips as she opened her chamber door and started for the dinner room.

When the three of them entered the dining chamber, William stood. His tanned face was illuminated by two large chandeliers suspended above the table and three candelabrums which formed a line from the table's head to foot.

"You're looking very fit," she said by way of greeting him. Then, tossing a glance at her true sister, she added. "Permit me, Mr. Birmingham, to introduce you to my sister . . ." She caught herself just before she blurted out *Maryann*. "Theodora."

He was sure to think she was lying again for the two sisters looked nothing alike.

"I hope you're comfortable, Miss Door," he said to Maryann. "You don't have to share a chamber with your sister. It would be no trouble to put you up in another room. A room of your own."

All of Maryann's former haughtiness vanished like whiffs of smoke. She smiled. "That's very kind of you, Mr. Birmingham, but I'm comfortable with my sister. In a strange house, it's good to have something familiar."

He nodded, staring at Maryann for a moment. "At first I thought your sister might be deceiving me—something at which she is most adept—but now I do see a resemblance. It's in your mouth. Your upper lip is almost exactly like Isadore's."

It was true. Few people ever noticed that the two disparate sisters shared the Beresford mouth. Sophia was flattered that he knew her face so well after so short an acquaintance. More than that, when she had heard her first name on his lips she had allowed herself to remember that night—and the following morning—when her name on his lips had sounded like a lover's endearment.

The ladies sat, then William returned to his seat at the head of the table. Sophia was at his right. "My dear Mr. Birmingham, I owe you my profound thanks for the cloak. It's not only much needed, but it is also lovely. I do hope you did not select it yourself for I would be distressed to learn you left the house after I implored you not to leave before making a full recovery." She gathered the crimson velvet about her neck and stroked its softness.

"I did not make the selection. My footman did. You must thank him."

"I am especially moved by your thoughtfulness."

"It was nothing. You know I'm a very wealthy man."

"I'm happy you were able to stay home today."

"If I have no setback, I shall conduct some business tomorrow, but I have learned my lesson about riding my horse on frigid winter days. I'll take the coach."

Maryann, who sat at William's left and across from Sophia, could not remove her admiring gaze from their host. Nor could she repress a smile.

It sickened Sophia to realize Maryann was available for courting.

And Sophia was not. She could weep.

"Did you finish your letters this afternoon?" Sophia asked him as she sipped her claret.

"No. Since I'm staying home tonight, I'll finish them then."

Sophia's face fell. She had hoped to engage him in some sort of game, even though three made an odd number. A pity Dottie didn't know enough to attempt any form of play.

* * *

Later that night as he sat in his lonely library, he congratulated himself on his ability to turn his back on the temptation of Isadore. At the completion of dinner, he had wanted nothing more than to prolong their time together. How he had wanted to play three-handed whist or chess or something so that he could continue being near her. He'd fleetingly thought of their closeness the previous night. It was almost worth getting sick to be comforted by Isadore. How gentle and loving she had been.

His throat went dry. He should not have allowed her to stay here. He'd not reckoned on how painful her presence would be.

Tomorrow he would talk to her. He would tell her he could wait no longer for the bullion.

Then he could exchange one pain for another. It was almost unbearable to contemplate her complete loss. Like a limb with gangrene, healing could not commence until one was severed from the other.

* * *

She left the house before William the next day to meet Devere at Sir George Malvern's on Half Moon Street. Because William had said he needed the carriage today, she walked. Thankfully, she had the thick warm velvet cloak to keep her from being too bitterly cold. Wearing it gave her the illusion that William was close, that William must care for her. How thoughtful it had been of him to procure it for her. She owned no possession she valued more.

The walk to Half Moon Street took less than ten minutes.

Locating Sir George's house was easy because her brother's mud-splattered, crested coach was parked in front of it, and Devere sat inside it, waiting for her.

When he saw her, he disembarked. "The things I allow you to talk me into!" He shook his head. "Now I remember why I choose not to marry."

She slipped her arm into his. "Don't tell me you're afraid of allowing a woman to manipulate you."

"Fear has nothing to do with it. Does it not occur to you I've already got my hands full looking out for my two errant sisters?"

She smiled up at him as they strolled toward the front door of Number 2. "You're a dear brother, and I'm very grateful to have you. Which reminds me, have you any word from your solicitor about my . . ." She turned up her nose in disgust. "Marriage?"

He shook his head solemnly. "But I received a strange letter from Finkel. It didn't mention you but said he would have your maid arrested for stealing his valuable valise. He wants it returned to him immediately."

"How very odd. I told Dottie to take it because it looked like rubbish."

"He's obviously anxious to have it back."

They climbed two steps and he rapped at the shiny black door.

Her chest tightened. *This has to be successful.* If it wasn't, she would have to break into Finkie's house. Which was almost as terrifying as Maryann's preference of leaping from the dome of St. Paul's.

The dark-haired butler opened the door and spoke first. "Lord Devere?"

Her brother nodded.

"Sir George is expecting you. Do come in."

Once inside, they divested themselves of their heavy outer clothing, handing them to the butler. A lump lodged in her throat as she looked at the velvet cloak William had bought her.

This narrow house was about the same width as William's, but it was not decorated with the same level of good taste. Where William's entry hall was floored in marble, this one was constructed of wood. The art work at William's came from the brushes of European masters while the paintings on Sir George's walls were portraits of Malvern ancestors by lesser artists. Everything at William's was freshly painted and polished and in perfect condition—as bespoke the house's purpose of showcasing his collections.

Sir George's house, on the other hand, had a cozy quality to it. Not only was a woman's hand evident, but this also had the look of a house where children had been raised. Her stomach knotted when she thought of the son who was now dead, the son who indirectly had brought them here today.

The butler showed them to the drawing room. This was evidently the pride of the Malverns, for it was furnished in opulent gilded furniture in the French style. The sofa and chairs were covered in bright pink and green silks that were beginning to wear thin. Such a baroque look was incongruous with the house's other dark furniture and scuffed wooden floors.

Since Sophia was uncertain what her role would be this afternoon, she lowered herself onto the chamber's most modest chair while her brother sat in a throne-like chair near the fire.

At least this house was warmer than William's. Even though she sat fairly near a window, none of the day's chill seeped into her bones.

A moment later Sir George strolled into the chamber, a smile on his face and a welcoming tone in his voice. "Good day to you, my lord." His gaze flicked to Sophia, and his brow hiked.

"Sir George," Devere said, "I should like to present you to my sister, Lady Sophia. She and I have a personal matter we wish to discuss with you."

The baronet looked even more puzzled as he came to sit upon the sofa. "I am at your service, my lord."

Sophia had not met him before. She would judge his age to be around fifty. Though his hair remained a warm brown, it has thinned considerably. His clothing was well cut in a most conservative fashion. He'd likely worn this fine woolen jacket for at least ten years. While it wasn't the first stare of style, it was of a sufficient plainness to render it rather timeless.

Devere drew in a breath. "We have come into possession of highly sensitive information about a scheme propagated by an evil man. A member of our family was the victim of his blackmailing, and we have reason to believe that your family, too, was affected."

Sir George's eyes widened. "You know the man responsible for this?"

"We do," Devere said. "Lord Finkel used his position in Society—and other disreputable means of bribery—to learn of scandals that could destroy people's lives. He also used his relationship with Josiah Smith's newspaper to lever his threats of exposure."

"You say your family was affected too?"

Too. He was not denying his involvement.

Devere nodded grimly. "The man doesn't care how many lives he ruins—or threatens to ruin."

"That's why we've come to you," Sophia said softly. "You can help us stop him. He must be stopped."

"I don't see what I can do."

"I am not in a position to testify against the fiend. I must protect an unwed sister's reputation."

Sir George sighed. "I see. You think because my son is dead that I can come forward, that he can't be hurt anymore?"

Sophia nodded solemnly. "I know how difficult it will be, but don't you want to spare others from having to go through what you and your son suffered?"

"I nearly beggared myself to protect my son's integrity. I can't let his memory be tarnished."

"But your son wasn't a thief," Devere said. "He was only borrowing the money with the full intention of paying it back on the quarter. That's just the kind of lapse in judgment that Finkel preys upon."

Her eyes never leaving the baronet's, Sophia nodded. "If Lord Finkel is tried in the House of Lords, a man of your stature would be an ideal witness. You command respect. Your own reputation is unblemished. I doubt you'd even have to go into particulars of your son's alleged indiscretion."

Sir George shook his head emphatically. "I can't. I can't drag Harold's name through the mud. He had children, you know? I can't do that to his children, my grandchildren. His illness was already so hard on all of us."

Sophia had heard that he suffered from consumption. The poor fellow was just her age when it claimed his life.

"I want my grandchildren to know their father as the fine man he was."

She started to protest. She wanted to point out that Harold would have wanted his father to expose Finkel, but she could not say those things. She had to respect the father's wishes. The man had suffered enough.

Devere stood. "I'm sorry to have wasted your time."

Their host got to his feet and walked to the door with them. "Believe me, Lord Devere, I am grievously sorry that I cannot help in bringing that horrible man to justice."

Sophia directed an understanding nod at him.

On the way back to Grosvenor Square, she realized how futile today's visit with Sir George had been.

Now she would have to move to the last resort—a harrowing prospect.

Now she would have to break into Finkie's house.

$\mathcal{C}$hapter 15

He dined at home again. That blasted Isadore had left before him that morning, robbing him of the opportunity to talk to her, to give her an ultimatum about the gold. He kept telling himself that was the only reason he was here this evening. He had to talk to her.

But the moment she strolled into the dining room, he forgot all about the gold. He could not remove his gaze from her dark-haired beauty. She was stunning in red velvet. Hair the colour of rich coffee beans piled gracefully on her head, a few loose wisps spiraling along her elegant neck. From her neck it was only natural that he lazily perused her incredibly creamy skin as it dipped beneath the bodice where the plump swell of her breasts instantly aroused him.

He'd been with many beautiful women, but none compared to Isadore.

What a bleak day it would be when their venture was completed and she returned to her husband. He would never again gaze upon her feminine perfection. Something inside of him sank. He would never again gaze upon any woman who affected him as she did. It wasn't just her beauty. Or the softness of her melodious voice. Or her obvious intelligence. Not even her incredible lovemaking accounted for the way this woman dominated his thoughts and leeched into his heart. It was the combination of all those things with one extra component—she loved him. She'd never tried to hide the fact.

He believed nothing she had ever told him. Except that. *She loves me.* Was he the biggest fool in all of England to believe her?

He eyed her as she came to take the same seat she had sat in the night before. "What? No cloak tonight?" He strove for flippancy in his voice to disguise the devastating effect she had upon him.

She gave a little laugh as her dark eyes met his, and then they sat down. "I wore it last night to demonstrate to you my gratitude." She rubbed her arms. "Though I daresay I could use it tonight. Why is your house always so cold?"

"It's not *always* cold. I assure you it's rather pleasant on warm, sunny days."

She and Theodora both laughed.

He began to pour the wine as Isadore scooped a ladle of leek soup into her bowl, then passed it to Dorothea.

He made pleasantries with Theodora, but he really only wanted to speak to Isadore. Lying, cheating Isadore who still fascinated him. Theodora was a lovely young lady, but he had no interest in misses straight from the schoolroom. Alarmingly, he had no interest in any woman except Isadore.

"So you left the house today?" he said to her.

She nodded. "Thankful I was for my lovely new cloak. I was quite the best dressed lady in all of Mayfair."

She was avoiding telling him her destination. He hated like the devil to pry. "You surely must have been the only lady in Mayfair *walking* today in this beastly cold."

"There was that," she answered with a laugh and a shrug.

"I hope your mission pertained to the business agreement between us."

She hesitated a moment before responding. "Of course."

She's lying. "Then you have a date set for the delivery?"

Her shoulders slumped. "Not yet, but clearly it will be soon."

That was just what he wanted. Wasn't it?

He needed to bring closure to this maddening week. More than a week, actually, since she'd come into his life. Nine days. Nine days that had irrevocably changed his life. Closure, he knew, would be much more final than his persistent aching for this woman. How long before he could purge her from his mind and heart?

Isadore did her best to keep up a jaunty conversation, but neither he nor the shy Theodora made many contributions. He kept thinking that he needed to speak to her privately. Toward the end of the dinner, he asked, "Tell me, Miss Isadore, do you play chess?"

"Of course."

"I shouldn't like to exclude your sisters, but it's been a long while since I've played, and I find I very much want to tonight."

Isadore's face lit up like the chandeliers above their table. "I am so happy you'll be staying home tonight and even happier to be able to play chess with you. I give you fair warning that I'm going to beat you like a drum."

"Indeed, Mr. Birmingham," Theodora confirmed. "My sister always wins. Our elder brother gets very angry about it."

"And don't mind about Theodora," Isadore said. "She has promised to read to Dorothea tonight."

* * *

While Maryann quietly read one of Mr. Scott's novels to Dottie on one side of the drawing room, Sophia and William sat at a card table near the fire. "I asked Fenton to have this table moved near the fire since you're always complaining about my chilly house," he said.

"I give you my thanks, but I'm even more grateful that *you're* taking care not to get chilled. I worry you'll have a setback." She was finally free from the worry that had dogged her these past two days.

"I am a great deal more improved today than I was yesterday." He began to set up the chess board.

She watched his strong hands fingering the chess pieces. Though he wasn't a particularly tall man, his hands were twice the size of hers. Everything about him bespoke rugged masculinity. "Yes, I can hear it in your voice. And you only coughed three times at dinner tonight. A vast improvement."

He chuckled. "Surely you didn't count?"

"Of course I did. I take my nursing very seriously." She started to say, "I take *you* very seriously," but she had no right to offer him any hope they could ever be together.

After he set up the board, he offered to let her make the first move.

"Do you really want to play me at chess, or do you want to discuss the bullion?"

He smirked. "How is it you've come to know me so well in so short a time?"

"Because I've waited my whole lifetime for you."

Why in the blazes must she always speak so truthfully? Well, maybe not *always*. She had developed a talent for lying with the same facility as she blurted out her innermost thoughts.

Anger singed his face. "I don't want to hear that. Whatever may have happened between us happened because you lied and told me you were a maiden. I would never have allowed myself to even think about touching you had I known you were married."

"In the way in which maidens are measured, I *was* a maiden," she said in a somber voice. "You do believe I had never lain with another man?"

"God, Isadore, stop torturing me!" He pushed away from the chess table and went to the fire, turning his back on her as he faced it.

She was stunned. The anguish in his voice matched the anguish in her heart. *He does love me.* As she sat there watching his powerful back outlined in firelight, she went from elation to the lowest low. While at first she'd wanted to fly into his arms and once again proclaim her love, now that she had pondered her hopeless situation she knew it would only hurt him more.

She vowed to never hurt him again. She must allow him to heal.

William was too honorable a man to live with a woman legally wed to another, and she was trapped in a union recognized as a marriage by the laws of England—but never by her. She would topple herself from the dome of St. Paul's before she would live with the vile Lord Finkel. Even if splattering herself was a terrible way to depart this earth.

She finally rose and went to stand beside William. "I'm sorry, William. I shall limit our discussions to our mutual business—or to our quest for a means to bring the odious Lord Finkel to justice."

He did not meet her gaze but continued to stare into the flames, nodding. "Tomorrow's Thursday. Do you still want to go to Lord Finkel's?"

"It's not a question of wanting. I wish there were another way, but this is our best chance. We'll go tomorrow night. Have you found a way to get us in?"

He nodded. "No bribing necessary. Our family has our own what you might call a private army. I've enlisted their expertise, and one of them assures me he can get in any door or any window. Do you think you can sketch a floor plan for us?"

"Certainly."

* * *

When he and Isadore reached Lord Finkel's house the following night, the street was in almost total darkness. Four of his "soldiers" met him there, but they were so well trained he hadn't seen the men dressed in black until he disembarked from his carriage several houses away from Finkel's. They crept up to him without making a sound. "Lord Finkel's house is the one of white stone, the only one with two bow windows at the front," Whitcombe said. "According to the diagram the lady drew for us, one of those windows is to the morning room and the other to the dining chamber."

Arnold, who had been standing behind the shorter Whitcombe, stepped forward. "Since you believe the library is the chamber most likely to conceal what you're looking for, I've taken the liberty of removing the glass from one of its windows."

Whitcombe smiled. "And Ellerby—being the smallest—has climbed in and gone around to open the front door for ye."

William had full confidence that Ellerby had been as quiet as a mouse. The Birmingham soldiers were said to be the best trained in the world.

Nodding, William turned to Isadore. "Ready?"

"Yes," she whispered.

The two figures in black moved like felines toward the house with two bow windows. At his insistence, she had worn her old torn black cape. She followed him up the four steps to the front door. His hand settled on the knob, his heartbeat accelerating. What if it squeaked? What if they were greeted by armed men? He'd learned that Finkel's servants were not the run-of-the-mill domestic staff. They were cutthroats and felons and men who would not hesitate to kill a man for sixpence.

William and Whitcombe had discussed the possibility of exposure. Whitcombe had one of his men hiding on the ground floor to protect William and Isadore. The knowledge that one of his men was lurking there lessened William's anxiety. He'd told that man his first concern was to protect Isadore. "I can take care of myself," he'd said.

The door did make a muffled squeak as he eased it open just enough to turn sideways and enter. The hallway was in darkness. He stood there for a moment, listening. When he was assured that no servant had been alerted to his presence, he beckoned Isadore to enter.

Once she was in the house, she took charge. "Follow me," she whispered.

She walked to the end of the checkered

corridor. He knew from her floor plan, she was going to the library. Ellerby had purposely left the library door open for them. One less potential squeak.

When he reached the library, he slowly closed its door while she lit candles from the smoldering fire in the grate. They had to have light to conduct a search, especially a search for incriminating letters.

"The desk drawers stay locked," she whispered, "but I believe he keeps the key inside the Sevres urn on his mantel." She moved to the chimneypiece and carefully lifted the piece of fine porcelain.

He heard the scrape of metal against the urn as she withdrew the key.

She moved to him and placed the key in his outstretched hand. Then, without being told what to do, she lifted a candle and held it above the middle drawer as he slid the key into the lock. The drawer held a ledger and several pieces of correspondence.

He emptied the drawer's contents on top of the desk. She set down her candle, and they went to work opening each letter to gauge its relevance. The first one he opened was a tradesman's bill for servants' livery. He set it aside.

The next was a short letter from a former school chum asking Finkel for a loan of twenty guineas. William put that aside also.

"Any luck?" he asked her.

She shook her head. "Because he refused to have a secretary—likely because no decent man would ever stay here once he knew what measure of man his employer was—he has saddled himself with having to see to all the various bills from tradesmen. The greengrocer. The tailor. And many subscriptions."

They continued until they had looked at every scrap of paper in that drawer before William examined the ledger. It looked as if it had only been used for a week or two and held nothing of interest, and no large deposits of money had been notated.

After searching through the middle drawer, he examined the contents of the top right, and she the top left. Nothing incriminating. There were a pair of pouches containing much more money than even a wealthy man like William was accustomed to having. Interesting for a man whose estate was in shambles when he inherited.

It took no more than ten minutes for them to search the entire desk, and they did not find a single incriminating item.

"I suppose now we should start on the books," he said.

She gazed at the two walls that featured books from the floor to the high ceiling. "There must be a few thousand books here. It could take a week."

"Not the way I propose we do it."

Her brow arched in query as she eyed him.

"I feel no compulsion to leave the room as we found it."

Her face brightened. "I see. You mean for us to take a book at time and toss it to the floor after shaking it to see if anything falls out?"

"Exactly."

"Then I propose we get your Whitcombe and Arnold and all the fellows to help us. That will take no special skill. If they find loose papers, you and I can examine them."

"Excellent suggestion."

He merely walked to library window where Whitcombe had removed the pane and spoke to a man standing there. Within minutes, two of the men were in the library with them searching the books for letters or scraps of paper that might have been inserted into them.

A minute into the search, he knew he'd exercised poor judgment. Thumping the books to the floor was entirely too noisy. He had to instruct the others to stop and to begin taking out and replacing each book one at a time. Thank God they had help. This was going to take a long while.

The first twenty minutes were fruitless. Then Ellerby exclaimed in a husky whisper. "I've found something, guv'nah!"

William hurried to meet Ellerby as he came off the ladder and handed him a single piece of paper. Moving the candle, William read the first line and crumbled the piece of paper. *Gather ye rosebuds while ye may.* It was a copy of a Robert Herrick poem! He looked to the spine of the book it came from. It was a volume of Robert Herrick.

Both men climbed back on their respective ladders. With four of them working quickly, they were able to examine every book in the library in one hour.

And they found nothing.

He sighed. Isadore sighed.

"He's got to keep his *valuables* somewhere," William said.

"If only we knew where. Do you think he might have a locked box in his bedchamber?" she asked.

"It's possible. But your floor plan didn't include the bedchambers."

She shook her head. "I know not where his chamber is, but I do know that no one other than servants lives here. We would likely have the whole bedchamber floor to ourselves."

William's gaze flicked to the case clock upon the mantel. It was nearly four. "We can't risk it. He could come at any time now. Perhaps another time."

She shook her head. "We'll never have the chance again after he discovers tonight's break-in. He's known to be a vicious master to his servants. He will deal with them harshly for allowing this to happen. Rest assured, it can never happen again."

If she weren't with him, William would not hesitate to climb upstairs to Finkel's bedchamber, but he couldn't risk Isadore's safety. He shook his head. "No. We leave now."

Her head bent as she solemnly nodded.

* * *

Early the next afternoon, Sophia sat morosely peering from her bedchamber window. An hour earlier she had watched as William's coach came around to collect him. Another day she would not see him. She wondered if he would dine at home that night. She was so pitiable. She lived for each moment in his presence.

It was while she was contemplating her melancholy life that she watched a long cart pull up in front of William's house. It wasn't every day one saw postilions on horses pulling a cart. And these postilions were armed! Her gaze moved to the box where the coachman sat. He stepped down, then reached up to assist a lady. A well dressed lady who began to walk to William's door.

Isadore!

$\mathcal{C}$hapter 16

She had to get to the door before Fenton answered. Sophia quickly slid her feet into her slippers and raced from her bedchamber. Holding her skirts in her hand, she scurried down the stairs like one racing from fire. Fenton was slowly making his way across the marble entry hall. "Fenton! Allow me to get the door."

A puzzled look flashed across his face. "As you wish, miss."

She swept open the door, and there stood a well-dressed woman who appeared to be five or six years older than Sophia. Her hair was dark, her skin fair, and anyone who gazed upon her would find her beautiful.

"You are Isadore," Sophia stated.

There was a defiant tilt to the woman's head as she glared at the younger woman. "I wish to see Mr. William Birmingham and only Mr. Birmingham."

"I am privy to your dealings with Mr. Birmingham, who has authorized me to conclude your . . . transaction."

"If you know everything, then tell me the amount I am to receive from him."

"Eighty thousand."

The real Isadore cocked a brow, her eyes narrow. "You have it?"

"I wouldn't be dealing with you if I didn't. Do

you have the . . ." Sophia eyed the long cart.

Isadore nodded. "It's covered with a shell of red bricks. You may come and inspect."

Were they going to uncover a fortune in gold bullion right here in Grosvenor Square? How Sophia wished William were here to advise her. Where had he intended to take the gold? Even if she made the exchange, she couldn't allow all that gold to just sit there unprotected.

Isadore began to walk toward the cart. Sophia followed. When they reached it, Isadore lifted back a section of tarp to reveal neat rows of red brick. She lifted a single brick, and below it blocks of shiny gold sparkled in the sunlight. "Every layer beneath here is gold," Isadore said in a low voice as smooth as the finest brandy. "See for yourself. Pick any brick." She moved away.

Sophia walked around the cart. On the other side she randomly selected a brick, removed it, and eyed the sparkling gold beneath. She pulled that one out, and there was another gold block beneath it.

Satisfied, she circled the cart and came to stand beside the beautiful Isadore, thankful that William wasn't here. There was something about Isadore that indicated she would be far more in her element around men. Was it the immodest scoop of her neckline? Or the sultry timbre of her voice? Whatever it was, Sophia would rather that William never be snared by the real Isadore.

Though it should not matter since Sophia could never have him.

It was then that she remembered Isadore was married. What husband would permit his wife to be involved in illegal schemes like this?

"How do I know that you're trustworthy?"

Sophia asked. "I could give you the money, and after you left, discover the bottom of that wagon is nothing but red brick. Mr. Birmingham has never before dealt with you."

"Mr. Birmingham may not have ever met me before, but Mr. Birmingham trusts MacIver, and MacIver knows I am an honest woman in a dishonest profession."

Those words could describe William. *An honest man in a dishonest profession.*

"I have fulfilled my part. Now I should like my compensation."

"I have the money in a large valise. You'll not be able to carry it by yourself. Perhaps your coachman can lend a hand. He looks to be a burly fellow.'

For the first time, a smile lifted Isadore's perfect lips. "My coachman is a most handy man to have around."

What danger the woman must court! Would her muscular coachman and armed postillions be enough to guard so valuable a cargo? Sophia swallowed. How would a complete novice like herself protect this delivery until she could get it to William?

She prayed he would come home soon. Very soon.

"I have your money here if you two would like to follow me upstairs."

* * *

After Isadore had left with her money, leaving the horseless cart behind, Sophia knew she had to do anything she could to summon William. He must have a plan for storing the gold. She sent for Thompson.

He came to the sitting room off her bedchamber

where she and her two sisters sat. "Pray, Thompson, it's imperative I get in touch with Mr. Birmingham immediately. Do you know where he may be?" Sophia asked.

The tall servant stood there for a moment, staring at nothing as he tried to recall what his master had spoken of that morning. "I can't say that he told where he was going. If I were to guess, I would say he may have gone to the family's bank."

The bank? Did he need money? Perhaps he was getting the eighty thousand guineas with which to pay her brother. "And you know where this bank is?" she asked.

He nodded.

"Then you must go there at once and tell him I need him. It's urgent."

"Certainly, Madam."

Why had he called her madam? Just a short time ago Fenton had called her miss. William must confide in his valet. Just as Sophia always confided in Dottie. Did that mean William had bemoaned the fact the woman with whom he'd been intimate belonged to another?

"And if he's not there," Sophia said, "please use your knowledge of your master to help find him. I cannot stress to you enough how important it is that he come here as soon as possible."

"Very good, Mad . . ., er, Miss Door. I'll go there directly."

After he left, Maryann eyed her elder sister. "Have you considered that once Mr. Birmingham gets his gold, you won't be able to stay here any longer? And you say you won't go to Devere House. What - - -"

Before she could finish speaking, Sophia burst

into tears. Maryann moved so close Sophia could smell her light lavender scent. "Don't worry, dearest," Maryann crooned. "We'll find you a place where the vile Lord Finkel won't find you."

Sophia wailed. "I don't want to leave William. Once he has the gold, I'll have lost my usefulness to him." She thought of one way she would like to have been useful to him, but William was too decent to make love to another man's wife. He truly was *an honest man in a dishonest profession*, or *an honorable man in a dishonorable profession*. She sniffed deeply. Twice. "I will never see him again."

"And that means I won't ever again get to see me Mr. Thompson, never again hold hands with Mr. Thompson."

Maryann's eyes rounded. "What are you talking about?" she asked Dottie.

"Me and the valet have engaged in a flirtation. He's even kissed me."

"I've never known you to ever show an interest in a man before," Maryann said. "And I've known you since the day I was born."

"That's because I ain't never met a man before who was as 'andsome or appealing as my dear Mr. Thompson."

"Then we must think of a way to allow you and my sister to continue on here." Maryann switched her attention from Dottie to Sophia, who was attempting to pat away her tears. "Would it not be wonderful if Dottie and Mr. Thompson could . . . marry?"

Dottie's eyes widened.

Sophia's mouth gaped open. "I've never considered that. I cannot live without Dottie, and I daresay William feels the same about Thompson."

"So you need to marry William."

Sophia began to wail again.

"Oh, dear me," Maryann said. "I keep forgetting you're already married to that awful man. I suppose it would be too much to hope for his death? He's only in his thirties."

Maryann was voicing the same thoughts that Sophia herself had not been able to suppress. She had felt utterly guilty for wishing a fellow human being dead, but if someone deserved to die for his evil deeds, that man was Lord Finkel.

A pity it was that the wretched man would probably outlive them all.

And it was an even greater pity that she had ever married him.

Now Maryann started to cry. "It's all my fault that you're so miserable. I've ruined your life, and now I'm breaking Dottie's heart, too."

Sophia morosely nodded. "You and I have both acted impetuously, and now we're both paying for it. I pray, pet, that you put your indiscretion behind you, that you not allow it to ruin your life. I pray that in the future you will think long and hard before ever doing something you could not disclose in a conversation with our mother."

"If only there was some way to stop that odious Lord Finkel from ruining people's lives," Maryann said, sniffing as she wiped tears on her sleeve.

Sophia's face brightened. "Perhaps that's how I can continue staying here. I feel it in my bones that if we had enough time, William and I could find a way to crush Finkie."

"I'll do anything in my power to help."

* * *

It was after three before Thompson returned. He looked dejected. "I went everywhere I could think of, but I was not able to locate Mr. Birmingham."

In an hour it would be dark.

"Did he say if he would dine at home tonight?" Sophia asked.

"He said it was his intention to dine at home."

An ambiguous statement, to be sure.

She dismissed the valet, and the three ladies began to prepare for dinner.

She was disappointed she hadn't requested her clothes that remained at Devere House. It grew tiresome wearing the same things over and over. She would have had twice as many dresses did she not share half her trousseau with Dottie.

This night she again wore the red velvet. From the sultry expression in his eyes when she wore that gown, she knew William found her desirable in it.

While Dottie was pinning up her hair, she heard William's step in the outer corridor. She had come to know so much of him—the fine blond hair on the back of his hands, the nobility of his character, the way his upper lip quirked when he was amused, the distinctive sound of his purposeful stride.

She did not know how she could bear it if she never again had the opportunity to observe those things, if she never again laid eyes on the man who'd been created for her.

She leapt from her dressing table and went to the door.

"But, milady, yer hair ain't properly dressed!" Dottie protested.

Ignoring her, Sophia flew into the corridor.

He was almost to his chamber door and turned to regard her. Her heated gaze took in his complete masculinity. He wore Hessians and buff breeches and brown woolens that feathered together all the gold and tans that distinguished him from all other Englishmen she knew. A tuft of his hair casually dipped against his forehead. Despite that he was a gentleman, she'd never known a more rugged man. He was such a paradox.

Instinctively, she knew there was something about him she did not know, just as there was much about her he did not know. It mattered not. They had been put on earth for one another.

As he lazily perused her, her breath stilled. "You look lovely, madam."

How she hated being addressed as madam, as the wife of another man. What a cruel fate had been dealt her. "I've been trying all day to reach you."

His brows lowered. "Is something wrong?"

"The gold's here."

His eyes flashed with some expression. Was it satisfaction? Or was it disappointment? "What do you mean *here*?"

"Did you not see a cart in front of your house just now?"

"I did not."

Perhaps his mind had still been occupied with whatever it was he'd been doing that day. That must explain why he'd not noticed the cart. Or perhaps he absently thought the cart belonged to the adjoining house. Since his house was so narrow, the space in front of the houses on either side could easily encroach on his.

"Come, I'll show you," she said.

He offered her his crooked arm, and they began to descend the stairs. When they reached the marble foyer and started for the outer door, one of the footmen rushed to open it for them. "Won't you be needing yer coat, Mr. Birmingham?" the youthful footman asked.

William shook his head. "No, we're just taking a quick look outside." William let her exit first.

She was smiling.

Until she saw the cart was gone. Eighty thousand pounds of her brother's money—money she had promised to rapidly repay—had vanished.

$\mathcal{C}$hapter 17

He'd trusted her. He'd known she was a lying, scheming, law-breaking cheat, but he'd believed in her inherent honesty.

Now he'd discovered another of her talents. The woman was a skilled actress. She was most convincing in her surprise that the supposed cart of gold was gone. What new mischief was the woman conceiving?

There were tears in her eyes and a tremble in her voice. "Oh, my God! I swear to you, it was here! I examined the gold myself. It was hidden beneath a shell of red bricks. How could someone just take it away?"

His expression inscrutable, he spoke casually. "Were there horses?"

She shook her head. "When the delivery was made, there were four horses ridden by armed postillions. When my . . . my *contact* left, the horses were untethered, and the four postillions rode off.

"I sent Thompson all over London to find you. You needed to get the gold to your final destination. I didn't like the idea of leaving it unprotected." She drew in a ragged breath. "And it seems my fears were justified." Her voice trailed as she fought off tears. "I must have that eighty thousand! You can't know how desperately I need it."

Under normal circumstances, William might be more sympathetic to a crying woman. But Isadore had tried him one too many times. He should never have trusted her in the first place.

He strove to keep the anger from his voice. "Madam, this is not my problem. It's you, not I, who is out a great deal of money. I have only your word for it the cart was delivered here today, and your word is not worth a farthing."

Her dark lashes lowered as she winced. "But MacIver will vouch for my honesty. Does he not say I'm an honest woman in a dishonest profession?"

It was true that MacIver trusted this woman. And William trusted MacIver. They had worked together for several years, and MacIver, too, had proven to be an honest man in a dishonest profession.

"Please William," she whimpered. "You must help me get the gold back. Did you not say you employ a virtual army of highly trained soldiers? Can they not help us find the gold?"

It suddenly occurred to him that she had nothing to gain by faking a heist of the gold. She had not yet gotten paid for it, and she had likely expended a small fortune to procure the gold in the first place.

He was beginning to believe someone may have betrayed her. He slowly nodded. "I'll send for the General tonight."

* * *

She did not touch her food at dinner. She was far too upset. They had to get back the gold. She had to get the eighty thousand from William to give to her brother. Devere would be ruined if she couldn't replace the money in a matter of days.

The panic she'd experienced when she first discovered the cart missing briefly vanished as she looked to the park in the center of Grosvenor Square. Surely the Bow Street runner had seen everything.

When she saw no one there, she realized her brother had hired a runner to protect the valise containing his eighty thousand guineas. Once the runner saw the exchange, saw Sophia hand off the valise, the runner's job was done.

Her sense of devastation returned.

William attempted to keep up the dinner table conversation, but she was too solemn, too distracted to contribute.

Was Isadore behind the theft? Who else could have known about the exchange? Was MacIver really trustworthy? Was this shipment not the largest William had ever requisitioned? When one was dealing with that much money, even normally reliable men could turn corrupt.

She found herself wondering if a neighbor on Grosvenor Square might have been looking out the window at the precise time Sophia was removing the outer bricks, examining the gold. Anyone watching would have seen the postillions ride off on the horses, leaving the gold-laden cart for the taking. It would have been child's play to hitch a pair of horses to the cart and ride off.

To where? She sighed. She did so hope that William's General would be able to unravel all of this and locate the scoundrel or scoundrels responsible for the theft.

As the others were finishing dinner, Fenton told William the General had arrived. Sophia threw down her fork and stood facing her host. "Please, will you permit me to speak with him?" It was a pity she could not be entirely honest with either the General or with William. She could not let it be known that the delivery was orchestrated by the real Isadore.

Sophia was so desperate to get back the gold, collect her eighty thousand, and return the money to Devere that she had fleetingly considered revealing her true identity. But that she could not do. Were she to disavow being Isadore, William would send her packing immediately.

She wasn't ready to put this chapter of her life behind her. Loss of William was the only thing that had the power to break her heart and make her weep. Other things—like losing her brother's eighty thousand—made her angry and sad and caused her voice to shake and her eyes to mist, but not to cry.

Since she was ten she had only ever cried since coming here to Grosvenor Square and discovering the only man to whom she could ever give her heart. Even though she knew the impossibility of dissolving her marriage, the unlikelihood of ever holding William's heart, she had not the strength to sever that which bound her to him, even if it were only temporarily.

William stood and nodded at her. "Come. Let us go to the library."

The General was a giant of a man. He must have stopped growing when he reached the midway point between six foot and seven foot tall, and every inch of him appeared to be rock-hard muscles. He greeted William with the congeniality of a long-time friend, though it was clear that he was in a subordinate position to the well-dressed gentleman who owned this fine home on Grosvenor Square.

"You remember about that sizeable shipment of gold I was expecting?" William asked the General.

"Me and the fellows have been at the ready for it for more than a week."

"It was brought here today when I was not here. It's been stolen."

The big man's jaw dropped. "That's terrible!"

"I have confidence if anyone can find it and restore it to me, that man is you."

The General's eyes flashed, then he hung his head. "Thank you, Mr. Birmingham, for your confidence in me."

William met Sophia's gaze. "This lady examined the delivery and can tell you everything she knows."

Sophia nodded. How she wished she could tell the entire truth, that scheming Isadore had been the one making the delivery. But that was out of the question.

Throughout dinner Sophia had been planning what she would tell the General if she had the opportunity to talk to him. "As you must know, General," she said, "people who deal in the type of . . . *transactions* that I do rarely use their true names. We know not where these . . . *colleagues* live, so the information I can furnish is as shadowy as our activities. Even when we wish to reach one another, we go through a long chain of contacts."

She sighed and went on. "Because I have practiced these habits for several years, I trust the people I work with."

"When eighty thousand guineas are at stake, it's best to trust no one," the General said.

"But Mr. Birmingham trusts you and your . . . *soldiers*, does he not?" she challenged.

"Ye've got me there, Miss! But all of the Birmingham employees are loyal because Mr. Birmingham compensates us handsomely."

She looked admiringly at William, then continued. "Before I suspect any of my *colleagues*, I would like to suggest that the culprit *could* be one of Mr. Birmingham's Grosvenor Square neighbors. We did make the exchange in broad daylight, and had someone been watching from a window, they may have seen me uncover the gold."

"Can you give me a description of the conveyance and of your actual exchange?"

"Yes. The gold was brought in a cart that appeared to be a load of bricks."

"What size was the cart?" the General asked.

"It was larger than average but not as long as some I've seen carrying slabs of marble. I would estimate it was about ten feet in length—the bed of it, that is." She peered at William. "Would you not say the bed of an average cart is but five or six feet in length?"

William nodded. "Was it constructed of metal or wood?"

"Wood. Rather crude looking. I suppose that's why the people I deal with did not mind leaving the entire cart here. It couldn't have been of much value."

"How was the gold hidden?" the General asked.

"There was an outer shell of red brick."

"Old or new brick?" he asked.

"New. The edges were sharp and straight."

"How many layers?"

"Just one layer of the red brick. Beneath it appeared to be all gold." She realized that while she had told William about the delivery, she hadn't explained it to the General. "You see when it was delivered, the cart was pulled by four horses, each with an armed postillion. When the exchange was complete, they simply unhitched the horses, removed the harnessing, and rode off."

"Do you think these riders were from London?" the General asked.

She shrugged. "It's impossible for me to say."

"You've given me enough to start on." The General turned to William. "Immediately."

Sophia set a hand to his sleeve. "I pray that you're as good as Mr. Birmingham says. If you don't find it . . . not only will I be ruined, but also a person who's very dear to me." She could not bear the thought of telling her brother about the loss. It would crush him.

* * *

William stayed in his library after the General left. He refused to sit before a chess table with bewitching Isadore.

Why was it he always ended up believing her? After all she had done, he was still vulnerable to beautiful Isadore.

Eighty thousand guineas was a lot to lose. Such a loss would diminish even the Birmingham coffers—and their family was the wealthiest in England. He hated to tell Adam about the theft. They already had buyers for the gold.

As he sat there near the fire he could not quit thinking about Isadore's parting words to the General. *A person who's very dear to me.* Did she have another lover? What did he mean *another*? William was most certainly *not* her lover. Though they *had* been lovers. The very thought of that one exquisite night with her was like a vise around his heart.

Had she been referring to Lord Evers when she spoke of *a person who's very dear to me*? But had she not told William there was nothing between her and the man to whom she was married?

For a long time he stared at the flickering orange flames.

And cursed the night Isadore had stormed into his life.

* * *

Finkel was playing faro at White's when Nicholas and Adam Birmingham strolled into the room. He'd been told Lord Agar had put them up for membership. How much had Agar received from the Birminghams to marry their mousy sister? The Cit had been tolerable enough looking, and it was said that nothing about her belied her origins. But, still. . . it was a rare occurrence for an earl to marry one of so inferior lineage.

Finkel watched the taller-than-average men and stiffened. He shouldn't be uncomfortable in their presence. After all, he was a peer of the realm, and they were mere Cits, albeit the wealthiest Cits in all of England. Nevertheless, they made him uncomfortable, especially after the way he'd embarrassed himself in their presence a few days earlier.

The men might be Cits, but they were welcomed with something akin to open arms whenever they entered the domain of the wealthiest men in the kingdom. The two Birmingham siblings who had wed had both married into the aristocracy. Finkel wondered if, like his siblings, Adam Birmingham was holding out for an aristocratic wife.

The thought of an aristocratic wife rudely brought him back to his own dilemma. Where in the hell was that wench he'd married? Even more importantly, where was his valise? He'd gladly strangle that skinny hag who served as Lady Sophia's maid for stealing it. His entire body stiffened, and his hands fisted. He would take enormous pleasure in strangling Lady Sophia, too.

"It's said the three Birmingham brothers can have any woman in the kingdom," his companion, Lord Percival, said.

Finkel whirled to Percival. "Three?"

"One doesn't see the youngest much. He spends a great deal of time on the Continent. I've met him. They're all a handsome lot, though he looks different from his brothers."

Finkel's eyes narrowed. "And when this youngest brother is in England, where does he reside?"

"His house in not so grand as Nicholas Birmingham's on Piccadilly, but he's got a fine house on Grosvenor Square."

Chapter 18

"I be so tired of sittin' around this house with nothing to do," Dottie said. "It be so pretty a day. Can we not at least go walk for a spell in the park at the center of the square?"

"Oh, yes, please," Maryann asked Sophia hopefully.

"I will own, that does sound good." Sophia's gaze flicked to the window in her sitting room. "It's so nice that the rain has gone away. Let us don muffs and cloaks and do the very thing Dottie suggested."

"I only wish me Mr. Thompson were coming," Dottie said with a little frown.

Sophia directed a sympathetic look at her maid. She did so understand how Dottie craved being with her Mr. Thompson, for Sophia felt the same about his master. How she wished she could intrude into his library where he was locked away. "I shall have to think of a way to throw you two together. Perhaps Maryann can help me plan something."

As they strolled along the plot of green, she eyed the various houses, wondering if residents of one of them had stolen the gold.

"What will we do if Auntie sees us?" Maryann asked.

Sophia's worried gaze darted to her aunt's house. How mortified she would be if that kinswoman discovered her here. She had almost forgotten Aunt Gresham lived across the street from William. "Oh, dear, we must return to Mr. Birmingham's at once. Even if Auntie could keep quiet after identifying us, her servants would be sure to blather, and then William would find out, and I cannot allow that to happen." She raced to the gate.

Two deeply disappointed females followed her back to his house.

Sophia had the odd feeling that she was being watched, but when she glanced to the South Audley entrance to the square, she saw no one. Then she turned to look at the Duke Street entrance. Nothing. She satisfied herself the mysterious thief must still be watching from one of the neighboring windows.

As the ladies were divesting themselves of their outerwear in William's entry hall, the door burst open. Sophia whirled around to face a band of six men – sinister looking, all of them. Her first thought was that these were the same men who had stolen the gold.

Then she recognized one of the men.

He was one of Lord Finkel's servants. *He's sent them to get me.* Her heart thundered in her chest.

The young footmen attempted to confront the men, and one of them ruthlessly butted his musket into the gangly lad, knocking him to the floor.

The library door banged open and William charged into the hallway. "What's going on?" His stricken gaze went from Sophia to the intruders. He froze.

The man in the center directed his musket at William. "I'll jest relieve ye of two of these women,

Mr. Birmingham." The man's glance moved from Dorothea to settle on Sophia, and he smiled. His teeth were rotten.

Afraid William would be killed trying to do something heroic, Sophia spun around to face him. "It's all right. I must return to my husband. Please don't try to overpower these men. I shouldn't like to see you killed."

She moved toward the man wielding the musket. Then her silent sister joined her. Maryann stood near the stairs, weeping.

"One more thing, milady," the gang's leader said. "We'll be needin' that valise you stole from his lordship."

The banged-up valise? It was a wonder she and Dottie hadn't thrown it out since it was so shabby. Then she stiffened. Hadn't Devere told her that Finkie was keen to get his hands on the valise?

All of a sudden, she knew where the vile man kept his incriminating papers. That explained why he had kept it in his library. She had to think of a way to convey this information to William.

She must try to make them believe the valise in her room was the one Finkie wanted. She tried to gather her poise. "You'll find the valise upstairs in the second room on the left, the Blue Room."

Her room.

A minute later one of the men returned with a dark green valise. She prayed none of the men remembered what Finkie's looked like.

"Before you take me away, sir," Isadore said to the man with rotten teeth, "I beg that you allow me to kiss my lover good-bye. I promise to go quietly after that."

The swarthy man peered from her to William, then he nodded.

William looked puzzled as she moved to him, her back to the men. She came so close he unconsciously drew her into his arms and began to lower his head. Just before his lips brushed across hers, she whispered. "You must get the valise from Dorothea's room. Lord Finkel must have hidden something there. Then, pray, round up your soldiers and get me away from Lord Finkel's." Her arms came around him, and she settled her lips upon his for a long, passionate kiss.

He looked stunned when she turned and walked away.

* * *

Once the door slammed behind the ruffians, Thompson, sword in hand, came rushing down the stairs. "They've taken away Miss Dorothea! No telling what those cutthroats will do to her."

William held up a halting hand. "We'll go after them. Just not now. Come with me to Miss Dorothea's bedchamber."

Thompson gave him a puzzled look.

"There's something in that chamber that will ensure the man responsible for the ladies' abduction will give them up."

In Miss Dorothea's chamber, beneath the high poster bed, they found a shabby gray valise. Even after all these days, it was still damp from the night they'd met at the Prickly Pig. How long had they trudged through the rain?

He opened it and noticed an even bulge under the lining on one side. "Pray, give me your penknife," he said to Thompson, who stood over him.

His servant proffered the instrument, and William used it to pry open the seam. He felt the heat of Thompson's body directly behind him, peering over his shoulder. The opened seam revealed a flattened pouch made of thin oilcloth that had been folded over in much the same way as foolscap. "What have we here?"

He unfolded the oilcloth, found three stacks of handwritten pages, many of them letters. He quickly scanned just a small portion of the first sheet. He felt disgustingly like a voyeur. Half a page was enough to tell him he was reading a torrid love letter, and the crest on the paper indicated the author was Lord Wakefield, a peer who held a high office in government. No doubt, the letter had been written to a woman who was *not* his highly respected wife.

"It appears the oilcloth protected these pages from the effects of the rain that night we were returning from Yorkshire," William said.

"I take it they're important?"

"They're worth a great deal of money to Finkel. He obviously needs these to blackmail at least a dozen people." Though he hated looking through such personal papers, he wished to find the one incriminating Isadore's sister and restore it to her. Twice he looked, but never saw the name Theodora. Nor did he see the name Isadore anywhere.

"When do we rescue the ladies?" Thompson asked.

"Very, very soon, my good man." He had to get Isadore away from that mad man. What if Finkel tried to force himself on her? It made William sick. "I've got to get to Finkel's before they discover they've got the wrong valise. You're to go to Nick and tell him everything. We'll need the soldiers. And have him put these in his safe." He handed

Thompson the oilcloth filled with papers. "Once I'm armed, I'll go out the front; you go out the back."

At least no one was watching his house from the square, William thought as he rounded the corner to the mews to get his horse, his senses alert. A knife was safely tucked into the specially made sheath inside his boot, and his hand cradled the hilt of the sword at his waist.

As he neared the livery stable, he slowed. Something was wrong. His mount should have been saddled by now and partially out of the darkened mews.

"Jonah?" he called out to his groom.

There was no response.

He stopped and drew his sword.

Just as three members of Finkel's "gang" stepped out, Rotten Teeth holding a dagger to Thompson's throat.

"If ye value yer man's life, ye'll drop that sword," the man with rotting teeth said.

* * *

As she entered Lord Finkel's house, the very same servants who had been tied with her dress sash the morning after she'd met William watched her through narrowed eyes. Now it was she who had her hands bound behind her.

"Some very disreputable men you employ, my lord," she said to their employer, her voice full of malice.

"That is exactly why I employ them, my dear." He stood in his drawing room, a glass of dark liquid in one hand and a satisfied look on his face. "How good it is to see you again, Lady Finkel."

"Don't call me by that odious name. I have no intentions of staying married to you."

"You'll not be getting away from me." His voice was guttural. "I *will* have my way with you, and I'll have your fortune, too."

"But you cannot want me now that I've been another man's lover."

He cursed and hurled his glass against the stone chimneypiece. "You will pay for that. You lover, of course, is William Birmingham, is it not?"

She thought of William Birmingham, of being his lover, and her heart softened. But she refused to discuss that fine man with the personification of evil who stood before her.

"I will crush him."

She laughed. "You're nothing but a weakling who has other men do his wicked deeds. Mr. Birmingham fights his own battles."

"I never said I'd crush him in an even fight." There was so much hatred in his voice and in his flashing black eyes that it frightened Sophia. She was sorry she'd involved William in her problems. Finkie could kill him.

Then she would either enter a convent or pitch herself from the top of St. Paul's.

Actually, splattering herself was infinitely preferable to bedding Finkel.

"You're not nearly as powerful as you think you are," she continued. "True, you manipulate people's lives, but you'll never have authority over me. I'll leave you the minute my hands are unbound."

He came closer, lowering his voice in a most sinister fashion. "Then, my dear, it appears I shall have to see that your hands stayed tied." His gaze flicked to the servant William had trounced that morning after they left the Prickly Pig. "Take Lady Finkel to my bedchamber, and have Frockmorton bring me the valise."

The brute came up from behind, closed burly arms around her so tightly it hurt, then began to lug her—kicking like a windmill—across the room, then up the stairs.

$\mathcal{C}$hapter 19

All William could think of was Isadore. He had to get to her, had to save her from being debauched by that worm Finkel. Yet he was powerless. He dropped the sword, and one of Rotten Teeth's underlings scurried to pick it up.

"I've held up my part," William said. "Now remove that dagger from my man's throat."

His gaze not leaving William's, Rotten Teeth moved the knife but did not sheath it. "Get in here," he said to William, a swing of his head pointing back into the mews.

It was so dark within, it was a moment before William saw that his groom had been bound and gagged.

Their captors set about roping his and Thompson's hands. A sense of hopelessness engulfed him. He could not bear to think of Finkel laying a finger on the beautiful Isadore, could not bear to think he might never see her again.

Damn but it was hard to believe he'd known her less than two weeks. She had gripped his heart so thoroughly he did not care if she *was* wed to another, he did not care if she smuggled gold bullion. All he cared about was loving her.

"What are your plans for us?" he asked Rotten Teeth.

"We've merely been instructed to keep ye out of his lordship's way until he can get out of Lunnon with the lady."

Had the man's sword plunged into him, William could not have felt more pain.

He'd never felt so impotent. The woman he loved was in grave danger, and he was unable to help her. Unless . . . "Well, then," William said, plopping down on a mat of fresh hay, "I believe my man and I will relax and wait."

Thompson knew what to do. They had been together so long they could almost read each other's thoughts. Thompson dropped into the hay beside him.

His idea must have sounded good to his captors because the three sat right down on the dirt floor just where the sunlight's line of demarcation fronted the stable.

The darkness of the stable was in William's favor. He waited a moment, waited for the men at the front to get caught up in a conversation, then he reached his hands into the top of his left boot. Given that his hands were tied at the wrists, it was a very tight squeeze, but his patience paid off a moment later when he unfastened his sheath and pulled out his knife. He cut Thompson's ropes, and Thompson took the knife and cut his.

Halfway between him and the captors, his sword gleamed on the stable floor. He knew if he dove for it, they would hear him, but it was risk he had to take.

For Isadore.

He whispered instructions to Thompson, who kept the knife.

Then he dove for the sword.

All three men leapt up at the sound, knives drawn.

But as they watched William, Thompson

disabled the man closest to him, which caused the others to flinch, giving William the split second he needed to lunge into Rotten Teeth—just as the man's knife came sailing toward William's chest. William dove for the man's feet, his own body slamming into the dirt floor with bruising force—and Rotten Teeth's knife grazing his back.

That William's sword had embedded into the other man's side rendered the man powerless to stop William from pummeling the third man until he begged him to stop.

With the three men writhing in the dirt, William instructed Thompson to tie them up, untie the groom, then head to Nick's. "Tell Nick everything. He must find the General and round up our men. I'm going to Finkel House to rescue the women."

* * *

The Finkel carriage was packed for a journey. That no-good devil must have designs on Isadore! William's heart started pumping, and a sickness settled in the pit of his stomach. He hoped to God he wasn't too late.

If only he'd been able to come with some of the Birmingham soldiers—not because he was afraid of facing these cutthroats alone, but he feared the chances of a lone man succeeding against Finkel's vicious brutes was very slim.

He hurried up the steps to Finkel's house and tried the door. To his surprise, it opened.

He was quickly met by a well-built butler who was considerably larger than William. William's gaze went from the butler to the morning room, along the entry hall and up the stairs. "I've come for Finkel."

The butler's eyes narrowed to slits and he spoke haughtily. "And you are?"

"The lady's lover."

"You must leave at once." The butler's genteel voice had taken on an accent of the lower classes. "His lordship's not in."

William stood there in Finkel's entry hall and yelled. "Are you here, Finkel?

William heard the pounding of feet above and saw Finkel looking down at him from the landing on the next floor.

"I believe I have in my possession something you want, Finkel." William held up the battered gray valise and began to mount the stairs.

"So you're William Birmingham."

He came face to face with Finkel. "If you wish the return of this valise, you must release the lady."

"I believe I'd be within my rights killing a man who tried to abduct my wife from her own house."

His words cut through William like a dagger. Suddenly, he remembered all that had transpired in the entry hall of his own house when Finkel's gang burst in. Isadore had said she must go to her husband. He remembered that Finkel had forced her into marriage. He remembered too that she knew this house well enough to draw a diagram. It made him sick. Was she married to Finkel, not to Lord Evers?

But MacIver was never wrong.

William's breath expelled, and an insincere smile tweaked at his mouth. "You cannot possibly be wed to the woman you abducted from my house."

"Lack of consummation does not nullify the fact that the woman is still my wife. I wed her almost two weeks ago." His dark eyes flashed wickedly. "Tonight she will be mine." He lunged toward

William. "I'll just take that valise."

"You may have it, but you'll never have her."

"I always get what I want."

William chuckled. "Including Lucy Mackenzie?"

Finkel froze. His face went ashen. "I know no Lucy Mackenzie."

"You lie. She's your legal wife. I saw the proof in Yorkshire two weeks ago. Just because you were but one and twenty and foolish does not negate the deed."

The very notion that Isadore was *not* a married woman made William feel as if he'd just drunk an entire bottle of champagne.

Finkel was silent for a moment. "That knowledge will die with you. Here and now." Finkel screamed as loud as he could for his minions. "Come and slay the intruder."

"There's a very big problem for you if something happens to me," William said.

"And what might that be?" Finkel sneered.

"My brother knows I was coming here. And he has in his possession something which will prove by what illegal methods you've been restoring the Finkel fortunes."

Finkel's gaze darted to the valise. "You found it. My oilskin pouch."

William nodded gravely. "By now it's in the Birmingham vault. I know everything, including by which means you trapped your. . .*wife* into marrying a reprobate like you. I. Will. Expose. You."

"Of all the families in England," Finkel said, shaking his head, his shoulders slumped, "it's my bloody misfortune to run up against the Birminghams, probably the only men in the kingdom who can't be bought."

"In that, you are correct." He came abreast of Finkel. "Where is she?"

Finkel tossed a defeated glance over his right shoulder.

William had to assure himself she was all right. Just as he started toward the room where he thought she was being held, he heard Finkel yell at his servants to ready the coach. "Never mind about Mr. Birmingham. We leave this moment!"

The first door William came to opened to a frilly lady's room, but Isadore was not there. He hoped to God Finkel hadn't been lying. Sighing, he went to the next room and pushed open the door.

It broke his heart to see her tied to a wooden chair.

* * *

She had prayed William would come before the vile Finkie did something thoroughly disgusting to her. How relieved she was. Now, she would neither have to join a convent nor splatter herself on the London pavement. She was so happy to see her beloved William she momentarily forgot about the rough ropes that scraped against her wrists.

William's eyes sparkled as he came closer, never removing his gaze from her. "I have a good mind to keep you tied up," he said lightly.

She presented him with a flirty smile as he bent to untie her. "You're too much the gentleman."

"How could you possibly know that?"

"I just do."

His hands stilled. He rested his full weight on his knees. Their faces were level, his eyes beginning to smolder. His proximity, his musky scent, his ruggedly handsome face were doing bubbly things to her.

She leaned into him, and he kissed her

hungrily. Sweet Heavens! Kissing William Birmingham was *the* most pleasant experience. How could she have missed out on something this wondrous her first seven and twenty years?

Because none of those previous suitors was William.

When the kiss ended, he settled his hands on either side of her face and looked at her—well, there was no other word for it—lovingly. "I don't like to think of you risking that lovely neck of yours. In fact, I have a proposal to make an honest woman of you." He drew her into his arms for another searing kiss.

"About that proposal?" she finally managed, a hopeful lilt to her voice.

"I don't know why in the blazes I should care one fig about you. You've done nothing but lie to me from the moment we met."

"My kiss was not a lie."

He pulled back and peered at her through narrowed eyes. "What about what you called me this afternoon?"

"When I told that awful man you were my lover?"

He nodded.

"That was not a lie, either."

"That settles it, then."

Her heart fluttered most agreeably. "Settles what?"

"I propose to make an honest woman out of you. No more smuggling."

"Actually, my dearest Mr. Birmingham, I'm not nearly as dishonest as you believe me to be."

"Enlighten me, please."

"I was so desperate to get away from Finkie that first night . . . " She drew a deep breath. "It was my . . . wedding night. I would have answered to any name."

"Then your name's not Isadore?"

She shook her head.

"You are well born, are you not?"

She nodded. "Until two weeks ago I had answered to the na milady Sophia Beresford for seven and twenty years."

He nuzzled soft kisses along the column of her neck. "I should prefer an entirely different name for you."

"Pray, what name would that be?" She circled her arms around him, her heartbeat galloping.

"Mrs. Birmingham?"

She started to bawl. This was no dainty weep. It was a full-fledged, open-mouthed, wail that originated deep in her chest like a spewing volcano and gave every indication it would never terminate.

"Pray, my dearest, why are you crying?"

She sniffed. She wiped her tears on her sleeve. She took his proffered handkerchief and blew her nose in a most UNdainty fashion. And she attempted to still the crying long enough to speak. "You know I cannot marry you. I am already married." This was followed by a whimper which lifted into another full-fledged wail.

"Then I'll just have to kill Lord Finkel."

She shook her head. "They'd hang you, and then I would have to throw myself from the dome of St. Paul's."

"Well, then, let me see. If you'd been honest to me that first night, you and I could have been spared much grief."

"How?"

"I had just come from Yorkshire where I learned

that Lord Finkel was already wed to a woman he deserted when he was a young man. Therefore, your marriage to Lord Finkel was never valid."

Her tears stopped as quickly as a hand clap. She threw her arms around him.

"There is one thing I should like to know," he said.

"I will forevermore be nothing but honest with you."

"Yesterday, when you were distressed about the stolen gold, you spoke of someone who was *very dear to you*."

"My brother, the Earl of Devere."

"I don't suppose his name is Dorian?"

She laughed. "No. His name is Alexander Beresford, the 7th Earl of Devere."

"There's more to your story."

She sighed. "Indeed. To start from that first night at the Prickly Pig, I knew then there was a special connection between you and me. And later . . . I knew I was in love with you. If I left Grosvenor Square I would never see you again. Even though I thought myself married, I could not give up my hope for some kind of union with you. My only hold on you was to be Isadore.

"I knew she would try to contact you and determined to intercept her. The only way that could succeed would be for me to give her eighty thousand in exchange for the gold. I begged my brother to get his hands on that enormous sum with the promise it would be paid back within a week."

"I see. Your brother's money is gone, and I can't pay for a delivery I didn't receive." He sighed. "This is a difficult situation. I have the eighty thousand, but it's not mine to just hand over to your brother. I'll have to discuss it with my brothers. But I vow I will not let your brother be destroyed."

"I suppose I need to accept your offer," she said. "I must reform your wicked ways. I shall use my dowry to help you financially because I beg that you never again involve yourself with smugglers."

He held her tightly and laughed, a deep raucous laugh.

"Pray, what is so funny?"

"You don't know who I am?"

"Of course I know who you are. You're Mr. William Birmingham, smuggler of gold bullion, my future husband, and the only man I could ever love."

He stood back and drew her hands into his. She felt incredibly secure.

"You've heard of Nicholas and Adam Birmingham?" he asked.

"Who hasn't? They're the wealth- - -" She stopped, suddenly realizing her great stupidity. "They're your brothers?"

His eyes laughing, he nodded.

"You're from *that* Birmingham family?"

"Sorry to disappoint."

"Why in the world do you resort to smuggling gold if you're that ridiculously wealthy?"

He shrugged. "A single man can take risks. I liked the excitement."

"Then I daresay you must marry." She moved into his arms. Nowhere on earth could ever feel better.

$\mathcal{C}$hapter 20

He stood there in what must have been Lady Finkel's bedchamber luxuriating in the feel of this woman he loved so dearly. His grip on her may have been too tight, but he was dazed by relief that he'd snatched her from Finkel's clutches barely in the nick of time. If he'd been minutes later, the consequences were unthinkable.

His head bent to hers once more when there was a loud commotion coming from downstairs. He drew back. "I hope it's Thompson with my brother."

They both raced toward the stairway.

From the marble entry hall, Nick looked up at him, his feet planted. "We got the weasel Finkel, or I should say the General and his men got him. We have to give statements to the magistrates. Those papers you sent in the oilskin packet are locked in my safe."

Thompson brushed past Nicholas Birmingham, peered up at his master, and spoke in a voice ripped by terror. "Where is Miss Dorothea?"

How remiss William had been to forget all about Isadore's . . . or Sophia's, elder sister.

"She's been tied up in a room on this floor, I believe," Sophia said. "Perhaps you can relieve her of the bindings."

The valet flew to the curved stairway and began to jump the steps two at a time.

"Do you think," Sophia whispered to William, "I should tell him she's my maid?"

William's brows shot up. "Why, you vixen!" Then he shook his head. "Let her be the one to tell him."

"Dottie's very loyal to me. I'd best go give her permission to speak."

"She speaks?"

Sophia shrugged. "Another lie, I'm afraid."

When he and Sophia arrived at the chamber where the maid was being held, Thompson was already on his knees untying her, crooning in a tender voice. "You'll be safe now, my dear Miss Door. I would die myself before I'd let anything happen to you."

Sophia's face softened as she watched the pair. "Everything's over now, dear Dottie. You may speak."

A look of shock registered on Dottie's face.

Thompson looked at the object of his affections as if she had turned purple.

The maid's face clouded. Her gaze dropped to her lap.

The valet's big hand curved along her slender face. "You can speak?"

She nodded.

"Then why do you look so wretched? If Finkel or his men have abused you, I will kill them."

Dottie shook her head but still did not look at Thompson. "I was not abused."

"Then what, love, is troubling you? Please don't tell me you're married to another?"

She shook her head again and tried to stand, but she couldn't get past Thompson's broad body.

Thompson got to his feet and helped her up.

"I've enjoyed these past two weeks, getting to

pretend I was a fine lady like Lady Sophia." Dottie glanced at Sophia. "I enjoyed your attentions, Mr. Thompson, but the pretending be over, and now I return to being a lady of no consequence."

"That is not true," he protested.

Tears gathered in Dottie's eyes as she strode toward the door. " milady, will you tell Mr. Thompson what I am?"

The poor woman, William thought. She did not think she deserved Thompson.

Sophia took her maid's hand. "But Dottie, you cannot be so cruel to Mr. Thompson. I'm to marry his master, so you and I will both be coming to live with them at Grosvenor Square."

Dottie's mouth gaped open. "How can you marry Mr. Birmingham when yer already married?"

Sophia beamed with happiness. "My marriage to Finkie was not legal because he was already married!"

The maid finally smiled. "I be ever so happy for ye. That Finkel was wicked through and through." Dottie drew a long breath and spoke just barely above a whisper. "I'd rather not be here when Mr. Thompson finds out what I am. I'll go to yer brother's and begin to pack our things for yer new home."

The thin creature slipped out the door as quietly as a flea.

Sophia peered at Thompson. "Allow me to introduce myself to you, Mr. Thompson. My true name is Lady Sophia Beresford. Dottie—whose true name *is* Dorothea—is my most beloved maid. A more capable servant does not exist."

William cleared his throat. "My good man, it appears Miss D . . . , er, Dottie, thinks you've been attracted to a fine lady and will be repulsed to know she's a mere maid."

Thompson could not respond for several moments. "I will own, sir, I am stunned. I truly took Miss . . . Dottie for a fine lady." He gave a bitter laugh. "Her muteness brought out protective instincts in me that I never knew I had."

Not the response William was hoping for. He'd been so happy that these two middle-aged souls had found love. He'd hoped Thompson would insist he loved the former mute no matter who she was.

Truth be told, William was disappointed in Thompson for the first time since they'd been together these ten years past. He gave his valet a nod, and the man left him alone with . . . Sophia. It was bloody difficult to think of her as anyone but Isadore.

"Well, my love, I have much to do now. I must give statements to the magistrates about Finkel. I must ask Lord Devere for your hand in marriage, and if he agrees, I must procure a special wedding license."

"My brother will agree. I'll go speak with him right now."

"He lives on Curzon Street?"

She nodded. "At Number 3."

"Then I will be there when I finish with the Finkel mess."

* * *

It was nearly dark when he arrived at Devere House. Since rains were threatening, he'd come in the coach, but his driver was unable to park directly in front of Number 3 because another conveyance was there.

Once he disembarked, he tossed a glance at the long cart in front of his coach. Good lord, it fit the description of the one the real Isadore had delivered to his house! He turned and went toward it, but a half a dozen men in red vests gathered around him. *Bow Street runners.*

"Lord Devere has given orders that no one's to come near this cart."

Nodding, he turned and strode to the door of the fine mansion at Number 3, hoping to God the cart was the one with his gold.

Sophia must have been watching for him. She came flying out the door. "Wonderful news, William!"

He eyed her mischievously. "You persuaded your brother to allow you to marry a Cit."

She came to take both his hands. "Well, that too."

He raised a single brow teasingly.

"Bless my brother, he was having me—or likely his eighty thousand quid—watched by a Bow Street runner who grew suspicious when he saw most unsavory looking men take off with your cart. So he followed. Once he had the destination, he reported to my brother, who authorized a half a dozen runners to restore the cart to us. Apparently one of Isadore's postillions got too greedy."

"That is wonderful news. About the Bow Street runners finding and returning it." He moved to his loyal coachman and spoke. "You need to find the General and have him gather up men and take this cart to Threadneedle Street. They know what they're to do."

Inside Devere House, which was much in the style of his own house but twice as large, Sophia's brother gave him a friendly greeting.

"He knows all about the wicked Lord Finkel's doings," she explained to William. "He and I were also working together to bring the odious man to justice."

"Then it appears, my lord, we have other things in common besides a high degree of concern for Lady Sophia's welfare and happiness," William said.

Smiling, Lord Devere nodded. "Won't you come to the library?"

They began to walk beneath a chandelier suspended high above the corridor which ran alongside the broad stairway. To his surprise, Sophia stayed at his side. Was he not supposed to meet privately with the earl to ask for her hand?

"I've got your eighty thousand, my lord. I shall never forget what lengths you went to for the woman I love. It could not have been easy."

Devere groaned. "You have no idea."

"Oh, but I do. You forget I've moved in banking circles my entire life."

"It appears," Devere said, "my sister's to marry one of the wealthiest men in the kingdom."

"My brothers and I have that distinction," William said. "Because my father was not an aristocrat, he was at liberty to settle his fortune equally among all three sons. As the youngest son, I'm well aware of my good fortune."

Sophia linked her arm through his. "Your enormous fortune, my love."

He patted her hand, then addressed Lord Devere. "Do I take it that you're sparing me from having to make a formal request for her hand?"

"When you know my sister as well as I do, you will know that when her mind is made up, nothing gets in her way. Besides, I trust her judgment. That shabbiness with Finkel was forced on her because she wanted to protect our sister."

William found much to admire in his prospective brother-in-law. He was especially pleased that Lady Sophia's brother didn't sound disappointed in her choice. William had prepared himself to be shunned by an arrogant earl, but Devere was not like that at all.

His eyes shimmering with warmth, Devere looked from one to the other. "We have already had marriage contracts drawn up for my sister."

Were they the ones she'd had for the marriage to Finkel? "I don't require a dowry, you know."

"Sophia thought you might say that."

She looked up at him admiringly. "I would prefer to pass my money on to my sister."

"Theodora?" William asked, tongue in cheek.

"Actually her name is- - -"

"Lady Maryann." He pulled a letter from inside the breast of his jacket and handed it to Devere. "From Finkel's stash. I thought you might want to burn it."

Devere took it, looked at it long enough to confirm it had been written by his youngest sister, then walked directly to the fire and tossed it into the flames.

"I will need your signature on documents that will protect Sophia in the event of your death or abandonment."

William went to the writing table, scanned the documents, then signed the last page. "I'm happy these were already drawn up. I will have the special license tomorrow, and I'd like to marry immediately."

"Me too," she said.

"I've never seen my sister like this. If there were such a thing, I would almost believe she's been taking a love potion, the transformation in her is so complete."

William felt as if he'd just grown a foot taller. "There is no more fortunate man in the kingdom than me." He smiled down at her.

* * *

She had sat in the church and softly cried as she watched Lady Sophia marry for the second time in as many weeks. Dottie had cried both times but for entirely different reasons. When her mistress had married Stinkie Finkie, she'd known it was a disaster. Today, she wept for joy. Lady Sophia and Mr. Birmingham were perfect for each other. She'd known it since that first night at the Prickly Pig.

The night she met Mr. Thompson, she thought ruefully.

How difficult it was going to be living in the same house with the only man she could ever love. She had given a great deal of thought as to how she would behave when she was near him and decided she would attempt to be as disinterested in him as she'd been in the upper servants at Devere House. None of them had ever turned her thoughts to kissing.

And other things.

Only one thing marred her mistress's wedding day. Rain.

After the wedding, while Lady Sophia and her bridegroom were being toasted at a wedding breakfast at Devere House, Dottie traveled a few blocks away to her mistress's new home. Lady Sophia had requested the coach for her long-serving maid to keep her from getting wet.

Rain turned Dottie's thoughts to those magical rainy days when she'd ridden alone in the coach with Mr. Thompson. When he thought she was a fine lady. How she longed to turn back the hands of time.

As the coach rounded the corner to Grosvenor Square, Dottie's stomach tightened. Mr. Thompson, who had sat at the back of the church at his master's wedding, was returning to the house. And getting very wet doing so.

She braced herself to act stiffly.

By the time the coach stopped and the coachman let down her step, Mr. Thompson was moving to the front door. When he heard the coach door open, he turned. Their gazes met and held.

Then he did a curious thing. He began to move to her. She was still within the coach.

When he got a foot away from the coach's steps, he stopped. Then he did something that was even more curious. He took off his voluminous black cloak and laid it in the puddles. "I shouldn't like to see the lady's slippers get muddy."

"Oh, I can't," she said.

"I insist."

"You'll take yer death of cold."

"I once told you I'd die for you."

Oh, my. Dottie hoped she didn't faint. She drew a breath and plopped her slender foot upon his sodden cloak. One step. Two. Three. Then she scurried toward the door. Though her thoughts were flying in different directions, she was still vaguely aware of how fiercely cold it was.

Inside the house, she waited to express her appreciation to him. Her satin slippers—a

castaway from Lady Sophia that were still
perfectly beautiful—were neither muddy nor wet
but only slightly damp.

He came striding in like a knight of yore,
handing the drenched cloak to a footman while
uttering directions on what to do with it. Then he
came to her. "My dear Dottie, I should like to take
the liberty of speaking to you in the library for a
moment."

They went to the library. She was shaking all
over and was quite sure she would truly be
incapable of speech.

He eased the door shut and came to stand
before her. "I wish to apologize for my appalling
manners yesterday. I had decided that I wished to
ask you for your hand in marriage for many
reasons, one of them being that I perceived you
needed me to take care of you. Because you were
not able to speak."

How Dottie wished to squeal with delight and
tell him she *did* want a big strong man like him to
take care of her. How difficult it was not to launch
herself into his arms.

"When Miss . . . that is, Lady Sophia said how
capable you were, I felt deflated, like you didn't
need me."

"Oh, but I do."

So she was able to talk, after all.

The corners of his mouth lifted. "Do you mean
that?"

She nodded.

"I must tell you it wasn't the fine clothes you
wore that engaged my affections. It was you. Your
small stature. Your sweet face. Your intoxicating
kisses. It was your face that I pictured every night
as I lay in my bed. Last night was torture." He

drew her into his arms and held her for a moment.

It was surely the happiest moment of her life. Then he lowered his head and kissed her with far more passion than previously. Then he held her some more.

"I don't even know what your last name is, my dear Dottie. Whatever it is, I should like to change it."

"It's not that bad a name, really. Not nearly so foolish as Door. Whatever would you change it to?"

"I've grown very fond of the name Thompson."

Then she realized how foolish she'd been and wondered if hearts could explode with happiness. "I have grown very fond of Mr. Thompson, and I should prefer your name above all others."

Once more he drew her into his arms. "There is no happier person in the kingdom than I."

"I believe I am. It's been a doubly blessed day for me, for my dear Lady Sophia has found her heart's desire. And so have I, my dear Mr. Thompson."

$\mathcal{C}$hapter 21

Darkness had fallen. Their hands were clasped, her head rested on his shoulder, and rain pelted against the roof of her husband's brand new coach. She tucked the rug more tightly to her chilled legs. "How much farther, my darling, to your brother's country home?"

He sighed. "We should have been there by now. Blasted rain." He dropped a kiss on top her head. "This isn't how I'd planned to spend our wedding night."

"Once we get to Adam's, all will be well. He sent staff ahead to ensure fires were built in every chamber." She began to trace slow circles upon his muscled thigh and rasped. "We will have the entire place all to ourselves."

Neither Dottie nor Thompson was to come. William had said assisting his wife into and out of her clothes was to be a pleasure reserved for himself.

"By the way, love, are you not going to read that letter you received from Thompson just before we left?" she asked.

"I'd forgotten about it." He took it from his pocket and began to read. Then he refolded the letter and restored it to his pocket, saying not a word.

"Well?" she queried.

"Thompson tells me he is taking time off from

his duties for an important occurrence."

"Did he tell you what the occurrence is?"

"He did."

She glared. "And . . . ?"

"He's to wed. I believe you are acquainted with the bride."

She began to squeal. "Give me that letter!"

He chuckled and gave it to her.

After she read it, she smiled from ear to ear. "Oh, my darling, this is the best day of my life. Dreams have come true for me and for my dear Dottie."

"And for your husband." He drew her into his arms for a tender kiss.

Since Adam's estate wasn't far from London— and since no one else would be there—it had seemed like the perfect place for their honeymoon.

"I shall instruct the servants to leave a tray of food on the floor outside my bedchamber door because, Mrs. Birmingham, I don't plan to leave the room all week."

"How curious it is that we think so much alike, my love."

"I knew we did that night when you knew Pope."

"What did you know?"

"That you were *THE* one. The one for me. The only one for me."

She effected a mock pout. "My taste in poetry is all that captivated you?"

He chuckled. "I know you are accustomed to having your beauty praised, but remember the night we met you looked as if you'd just swum the Channel."

"I must have been a most piteous sight."

He lovingly stroked the side of her face. "It

didn't take long before I realized you were possessed of stunning beauty. But that was only one of your many attractions."

"There are others?" She hoped that she had pleased him that one night in his arms.

He nodded and spoke in a husky whisper. "Why do you think I plan to spend an entire week in bed with you?"

She drew in a long breath. "I just lost my appetite. For food."

The rains started coming down even more fiercely. It was no longer the top of the coach getting the brunt of the hammering rains. Now howling winds drove the rain sideways.

"The last thing we need is for the coach to get stuck in mud," he said.

"I agree. We need to find a place to stop before that happens."

He conveyed that message to his bedraggled coachman.

Ten minutes later, they pulled into an inn yard.

"Allow me to go make the arrangements. I shall ask for the finest room." He took both her hands. "I'm sorry our wedding night will have to be spent at a coaching inn."

"As long as I'm with you, I will be the happiest woman in the kingdom." She lifted the hood of her red velvet cloak.

Five minutes later he returned. "I shall have to ask that you not show your beautiful face, my dearest."

Her brows lowered. "Why?"

He shrugged as he swept her into his arms and began to carry her from the coach. "Because the innkeeper may remember that on a previous visit I said you were my sister. Tonight I've said you're my wife."

That was when she saw the swinging sign for the Prickly Pig.

"Oh, dear. Will we have to use his private chambers again?"

"Thank God, no. It's early enough that we have been able to procure the largest suite."

William's coachman held open the inn's thick timber door, and William went straight for the narrow wooden staircase. She was careful to keep her head turned away from the populated rooms.

The chamber he brought her to was large, and it looked nothing like the cluttered chambers of the innkeeper. Best of all, it was warm. A wood fire blazed in its big stone hearth. The bottle of Madeira and two glasses he'd requested awaited them on a table next to the settee in front of the hearth.

He put her down, and she divested herself of her wet cloak. She was otherwise bone dry— thanks to her husband carrying her from the coach. She watched hungrily as he removed his sodden greatcoat, then the damp coat beneath it. When he sat to remove his boots, she went to her knees and assisted.

Then they stood, and she flowed into his arms like clay to its mold. "It seems almost incomprehensible that we met just two weeks ago beneath this very roof."

"I know. It seems as if you're a part of me, that we've always been together."

"It's fitting, I think, that we're back here for our wedding night. I fell in love with you here. I had not the slightest doubt of it even though I'd just met you."

"I realize now what I'd felt for Isadore that night

must have been love."

"Isadore?"

He held her tightly. "Do not be surprised, my lady, when you're a shrunken little white-haired woman and your husband is still calling you Isadore."

&pilogue

Six months later . . .

Sophia had been pacing the floor waiting for her husband to return. He had obtained one of the coveted seats in the House of Lords' gallery for the trial of the century. Today was the day the verdict would be handed down in the Lord Finkel trial. Every word spoken in the proceedings had been faithfully recorded, and there was scarcely a person in London who had not heard of the vile lord's reprehensible deeds or read of them in the many newspapers that reported on the trial.

When William finally came through the door, she was standing there. "Guilty?"

He nodded grimly.

"The punishment?"

"He's to hang until his death." He shrugged. "I confess when we went into this, I feared the lords would protect their own. I had not gauged how mightily those men detested his actions. And Devere was instrumental in swaying the more lenient lords."

"My brother has always commanded respect." She came to her husband and wrapped her arms around him as she nestled the side of her face into his chest. "I'm not sorry about Finkel. I had grown to hate him. He would have killed you that day at Finkel House to keep you from disclosing the existence of Lucy Mackenzie."

"And he would have done other things that don't bear contemplation."

She cringed. She would most definitely have splattered herself on the pavement beneath St. Paul's dome rather than subject herself to Finkie's embraces. And more.

"One good thing."

"What?" he asked.

"Were it not for the man's vileness, I would never have met you that night at the Prickly Pig."

"Then it seems I owe my happiness to the most hated man in all of England."

THE END

Author's Biography

A former journalist and English teacher, Cheryl Bolen sold her first book to Harlequin Historical in 1997. That book, *A Duke Deceived*, was a finalist for the Holt Medallion for Best First Book, and it netted her the title Notable New Author. Since then she has published more than 20 books with Kensington/Zebra, Love Inspired Historical and was Montlake launch author for Kindle Serials. As an independent author, she has broken into the top 5 on the *New York Times* and top 20 on the *USA Today* bestseller lists.

Her 2005 book *One Golden Ring* won the Holt Medallion for Best Historical, and her 2011 gothic historical *My Lord Wicked* was awarded Best Historical in the International Digital Awards, the same year one of her Christmas novellas was chosen as Best Historical Novella by Hearts Through History. Her books have been finalists for other awards, including the Daphne du Maurier, and have been translated into eight languages.

She invites readers to www.CherylBolen.com, or her blog, www.cherylsregencyramblings.wordpress.co or Facebook at https://www.facebook.com/pages/Cheryl-Bolen-Books/146842652076424.

9.99   5/9/16.

LONGWOOD PUBLIC LIBRARY
800 Middle Country Road
Middle Island, NY 11953
(631) 924-6400
mylpl.net

LIBRARY HOURS

Monday-Friday	9:30 a.m. - 9:00 p.m.
Saturday	9:30 a.m. - 5:00 p.m.
Sunday (Sept-June)	1:00 p.m. - 5:00 p.m.

31327338R20164

Made in the USA
Middletown, DE
30 April 2016